Elusive Dream

by
Ella Sailor

PublishAmerica
Baltimore

First printing

ISBN: 1-4137-3451-0
PUBLISHED BY PUBLISHAMERICA, LLLP
www.publishamerica.com
Baltimore

Printed in the United States of America

To Garrett Wilson
- lawyer
- mentor in things legal
- author
- friend

And to Dolores Goldstone
- notary public
- colleague in things legal
- friend

CHAPTER ONE

NIGHTWATCHMAN KILLED BY TEENAGE GANG: The headline screamed up at her from the morning paper. She scanned it quickly; another break-in computer fraud gone awry—three teenagers caught in the act. *The world has gone mad,* she concluded as she returned to her studies.

I really need to stop and make a sandwich, she decided, noting it was past the lunch hour. The discordant buzz of the phone cut through her thoughts.

"Hello, I'm looking for Miss Leanne Stevenson."

"This is Leanne."

"Miss Stevenson, this is Brett Walker; I'm a lawyer here in London. I understand from Judge Ben Davis that you are a very qualified young woman…looking for a position."

She waited. *Was this a statement or a question?*

"I…I…am needing an executive assistant."

"Judge Davis told you this? I'm sorry. You have caught me rather off guard. I will be looking for a position in the very near future…I hadn't really thought…actually, I'm really not a legal secretary…." She stumbled on, not quite sure what to say—certain only of her lack of coherence.

"I understand you have extensive experience in legal work…that you are familiar…."

"Well…I am familiar…I sort of grew up in my father's office; I worked with him…."

"Are you interested in coming for an interview?"

She paused. "How soon?"

"I have time right now. Can you come within the hour?"

Her lunch preparations laid aside, she showered quickly. *Oh, Lord,* she prayed, *help me know if this is part of the plan you have for me.* She reminded herself again of the promise in Jeremiah 29:11: *"For I know the plans I have for you…plans to prosper you and not to harm you, plans to give you hope and a future." Please, God, I need your direction here.*

What to wear? *Navy always looks professional…yes, the navy skirt and jacket…and the blouse with the green, white and navy stripes.*

*Brett Walker…Brett Walker…*she mused. *Why does that name sound familiar?* Suddenly, she knew! She took a moment to retrieve the morning paper. There it was. Brett Walker would represent the young offenders who murdered the night watchman.

"Excellent reporting," she muttered to no one in particular. "All found guilty without the inconvenience of a trial!" How her father would have exploded over a thing like that!

"Thank you for coming, Miss Stevenson." He motioned her to the chair in front of his desk. His gaze took in her professional dress, her confident bearing, courteous eye contact—beautiful grey-green, he noted in passing—short, dark hair swept back stylishly. She would be an asset to his outer office. *Sure hope she can use a computer.*

Handsome doesn't begin to cut it with this guy, she mused as she noted his six-foot physique…sandy hair…deep blue eyes…determined chin…deep tanned complexion. *You're buying trouble, Lee, if you think you can work here, and not lose it over this guy.*

"Now, I need to explain my circumstances," he began after brief formalities. "My assistant, Mrs. Beck, has asked to be relieved since her husband's cancer recurred; now she has been involved in a minor car accident that has left her badly shaken. I fear she will be unable to return and I'm in the throes of a criminal court case."

"I saw the morning paper; a trial hardly seems necessary." She grimaced.

"Yes...yes...so it goes. Now, do I understand correctly, you *are* looking for a position?"

"Well, yes...and no. I will be looking in the next couple of weeks, but I'm really not ready at this time...and I did mention that I have no formal training as a legal assistant...I just helped...."

"Judge Davis tells me that you are very qualified."

"He's terribly biased; he's known me since I was a child."

"So he knows you well?"

She smiled at his insistence.

"I take it you are competent on a computer? Windows? WordPerfect?"

"Yes...yes, of course."

"Do you have a resume?"

"No."

"Why is that?"

"I haven't needed to look for work...not since I was a teenager...and I'm really not sure what kind of a position...?"

"Would you be interested in working for me?"

"How soon do you need someone?"

"Can you stay right now? I'm really behind the eight-ball. I'm afraid I have quite a backlog."

She tried wildly to collect her thoughts. Stay?...right now? She still had a lot of material to cover before her final exam tomorrow night...she hadn't stopped for lunch...tonight was her night to help Brody on the computer. She hesitated.

"Would it be possible for you to work a few evenings this week?" he went on.

"No...no...not this week...well...not until Friday. I have classes on Tuesday and Thursday evenings; my week is full."

"Classes?"

"Yes...university."

"University? What are you studying?" His mind whirled, trying to make sense of her schedule...wondering why she wouldn't go in the daytime, since she obviously didn't do anything else.

"Well, actually, I'm in the midst of making some decisions. I haven't been satisfied with…I've just been questioning the direction my life has been taking."

"So," his voice held a slight edge, "you don't have a job, but you're not sure you want one? You're going to university, but you're not sure where you're heading? Do you have a problem making decisions, Miss Stevenson?"

"Just with the big things, Mr. Walker. I don't sweat the small stuff." She rose as she spoke.

"Would you mind to sit down?" he asked with a puzzled look on his face. "I'm not quite done."

"You *are* done, Mr. Walker," she smiled politely as she picked up her small handbag and headed for the door, "… *quite* done!"

"No…please…Miss Stevenson. I apologize. I hadn't meant that quite the way it came out." She paused in her move toward the door. "Can we try again?" he asked, motioning her toward the chair.

She hesitated as though uncertain what her choice should be.

"Please…."

She paused, then reluctantly re-seated herself. "Do you intend to swear me in before you proceed with the cross-examination?" she asked mischievously.

"I've already apologized for that," he countered. "Perhaps you might be generous enough to forgive."

"I don't know if I want to work for you, Mr. Walker, but I will certainly help you for a few weeks if that will make a difference…give you time to find an assistant. However, I can't work after five this week until Friday. Next week I should have Tuesday and Thursday evenings free."

"Thank you; I appreciate your willingness. Do you have any questions?"

"Yes. I would like to know something about you—what kind of law you practice—I take it you're a criminal lawyer? Are you married? Do you have a family?"

"No, no, and no. I am not a criminal lawyer, am not married, do not have a family. I've been quite successful in criminal cases in the past but have never considered criminal law exclusively. I'm defending these boys as a favour to an old friend; his son is one of the three."

She nodded, obviously satisfied.

"Shall we discuss your salary? What would you expect?"

"I'm not sure. I've never worked at a regular job. My father paid me by the hour since my hours were so erratic. Perhaps you'd like to wait and see…."

"And if I decided you weren't worth…."

"That would tell me something about *you*, Mr. Walker."

Clever little rascal, he thought, feeling just slightly intimidated. "What did your father pay you per hour?"

"Fifteen dollars."

"Would you be happy with that, until you decide if you want to be on regular salary?"

She nodded.

"Shall we begin then?" he asked. "Perhaps I need to show you the office."

"I'm sorry," she interjected, "but I was about to have my lunch when you called, and I'll need a sandwich. Have you eaten?"

"No…actually, I had forgotten. I haven't had anything since morning coffee."

"Shall I slip out and get some sandwiches?"

"Perhaps you might like to order from the deli downstairs…corned beef on rye for me. They're good about bringing it up. Just put it on my account."

While her computer warmed up, she busied herself in the small kitchenette. The coffee pot had long ago given up on a good scouring, and she proceeded to clean it thoroughly and put on a fresh pot before the sandwiches arrived. The cream in the fridge was past its prime and she called the deli again, asking for a fresh carton.

"How did you know I liked cream in my coffee?" he asked, surprised, as she served his sandwich and coffee.

"I presumed that under the green fuzz in the fridge…there must have been cream…and the cups in the sink…."

He laughed. "Will you join me?"

9

She hesitated, "If you wish."

"I wish."

This is going to be one interesting arrangement, he mused as she joined him at the small table near the window.

The next three and a half hours flew by as they worked together. She rose promptly at five and bid him a good day. "Shall I see you at eight in the morning, then?"

"That would be fine…and thank you…for your help today."

I'll need to call Dave and get some advice about this guy, she mused as she walked the two blocks to Brody's house, to help the disabled boy with his computer.

❧

"He's one mighty sharp cookie," her brother Dave responded to her question. "He instructed several of my classes a few years ago…doesn't leave any pebble unturned. He seems friendly on the surface, but they say nobody gets any further. Gossip says he's a woman hater…definitely not a womanizer…never dates…not a drinker. My guess is that he'd be okay to work for…you'll learn a lot. Just don't get too fond of him; he's one handsome rascal, but it's a dead-end."

"Well, everything I ever wanted to know in one paragraph," she said with a laugh. "He really is a little different…rather withdrawn…goal oriented; course he's really swamped right now with no secretary and this murder trial. Guess I told you that Judge Ben suggested he call me to give him a hand; I wouldn't have considered it otherwise. I'm really not ready to go to work yet…both of my final exams coming up this week."

"Well, take it easy, sis; don't let him push you further than you have time for. You've worked hard on these courses; you deserve to do well. Don't cheat yourself. I'll be home for the weekend and we'll talk. You'll have a feel for the office by then…whether you want to continue."

Chapter Two

"Can you cancel any appointments for this morning? I need to slip down to the jail," he announced as he headed for his office. "I should be back before noon."

"Yes, certainly." She looked questioningly at his flushed countenance. "Are you okay, Mr. Walker?"

"I'm not sure. Probably should have stayed in bed, but the rat race…." She heard a muffled crash as his chair skidded backward into the book shelf and he landed heavily on the floor.

"Oh, Mr. Walker! Mr. Walker!" *Now, Leanne*, she admonished herself, *get a grip! Call 9-1-1.* As if listening in on a stranger's conversation, she heard herself giving directions to the ambulance, reporting his pulse rate, and suggesting that his temperature was terribly high.

"Where will you take him?" she asked the ambulance attendants.

"University Hospital."

She sat stunned. Should she have gone along? Shouldn't she be notifying his next-of-kin? Shouldn't she call somebody? Yes…the prosecutor; preliminary hearing will have to be postponed. She dialled quickly and explained the situation to a startled prosecutor. *Now what? Who would know where to find his family? Judge Ben Davis? Yes, of course, he would know!*

"I'll be right over," she heard with relief. What a good friend the judge was, her dad's old law partner. She and Dave had called him *Uncle Ben* since they could remember. She was glad for his shoulder to lean on. The accident that took her mother's life over a year ago had left them all in a state of shock. Her father had survived...barely...and only weeks ago had succumbed to his injuries. And Uncle Ben had been there—caring, advising, watching over them like a guardian angel. And he had gotten her this job—a little prematurely, to be sure—but he probably felt it would help her make up her mind about the future.

Her thoughts continued to swirl as she waited for the judge. Well...she would do the best she could for Mr. Walker. She noted the huge backlog of files on his desk and decided she would check them out...deal with the pressing matters...postpone the rest. And the boys in jail? She should call the high school and do a background check...get some records: academics...sports...attitudes.... Better call the parents and get them to sign a consent for the school. It could be a busy day...along with a final exam in Criminal Law.

And Mr. Walker...he'll need some things when he regains consciousness—some personal stuff. She started a small list: toothbrush and paste, shampoo, hair brush, razor, pyjamas, bathrobe and slippers. Perhaps she'd slip home over the lunch hour; her dad's things were all there and in good repair. She had found Mr. Walker's keys on his desk but he'd probably take a dim view of her invading his privacy to get his own personal effects. What about his health card? Probably in his wallet; she'd ask Uncle Ben to go to the hospital and check on him. She would go herself tomorrow, if he was well enough for visitors. She hoped it wasn't anything serious...that horribly high temperature...could be meningitis. Worrying won't help. She whispered a prayer as she continued to make order out of the chaos around her.

"Mr. Walker's office," she answered the phone automatically, her mind still on the open file in front of her.

"Hello, this is Reverend Bill Somerville, from the Cornerstone Bible Church. Would it be possible to speak to Mr. Walker?"

"Hello, Pastor, this is Leanne Stevenson, and I'm helping Mr. Walker for a few days. Sorry, he isn't available; he just went to the hospital with a very high fever. Anything I can do to help?"

"Good to hear your voice, Lee. Makes me feel like we have an ally. I'm sorry to hear that Mr. Walker is in hospital. I'm wondering about the boys in jail? One of them, Gregg Romero, is from one of our church families. We are totally convinced that he is not involved and I have some evidence that may be of value. Is it possible to see this lawyer…in the hospital?"

"Oh, Mr. Somerville, you…uh…it will be a while before he's able to see anyone. He was unconscious when they took him from here a half hour ago. It's not likely he'll be up to having a visitor for a while. Could you…would you…come to the office and give me a statement? I hope to get as much background information on these boys as I can, so that Mr. Walker…."

"Leanne! Leanne! Leanne! I appreciate what you're trying to do, but you're acting as though Gregg is involved here. They have him in prison…he's missing school…his parents are beside themselves…."

"All of the parents would like to have their children out of jail, Pastor, but murder is a very serious charge, and the wheels of justice grind slowly. Unless the authorities have evidence to prove that Gregg is innocent, he'll have to stand trial…there will be no bail…."

"Will you let me know the earliest possible moment that Mr. Walker is available?"

"Yes, of course. Meantime, will you be kind enough to give us a statement. We will need something concrete to go on. Mr. Walker was not impressed with the Romero boy; he totally refused to co-operate…refused to answer questions. Will you come?"

"You're convinced that this will help?"

"Mr. Walker is a very busy man. It will get you a hearing with him, if your statement appears to be credible."

"Fine, then."

"Sounds like my special girl is in her element." The portly judge grinned as he bounced through the door. "Any word from the hospital?"

"No, and I'm wondering if they would even know who to call. I don't know if Mr. Walker had his wallet…his health card. I called and told them who he is and so on, but you know how easily that can get mislaid. Would you go over and make sure all is well?"

"Of course, of course."

"Actually, he'll need a few things when he comes to. Would you just run the ranch here for a few minutes while I trot off home and pick up some personal effects for him?"

He nodded as she grabbed her purse and keys and headed for the door.

It seemed only minutes before she returned with a sleek leather week-ender. "Dad's," she explained at the judge's questioning look. "I've put in a couple pairs of pyjamas, slippers, bathrobe, toiletries, etc. He can let you know if he needs anything else. Oh, yes, his keys and his cell phone." She smiled. "I'll be up to see him Wednesday after five. If he needs anything before then, he can call."

"I doubt they'll let him use the cell phone in the hospital, but we can see when I get there. Anything else?"

"Yes…oh, yes…what about next-of-kin? Is there someone…?"

"No one. Brett was an only child…orphaned, I understand. Painful childhood. I'm sure he has no connections."

"You'll let me know?"

"I'll call as soon as I find him. Thanks for your willingness to help him out. He really is quite an exceptional lawyer…actually quite exceptional all around."

❧

He opened heavy eyelids as the judge approached his bed. "Ben," he murmured, "is that really you?"

"You betcha! I was up to see you yesterday but you just weren't into visitors…or much of anything else. How's it going?"

"Not great. What day is it?"

"It's Wednesday morning. Guess you must have slept away 24 hours. Have they decided if you'll live?" he joked.

"Apparently I have a particularly virulent strain of influenza. They tell me I nearly died. Guess I was pretty dehydrated. How did I get in here?"

"Leanne called an ambulance when you blacked out. Your pulse and temperature were off the wall."

14

"What a time to take a week off. Those kids' parents will be frantic."

"They already are. Leanne has been handling things very well. I told you she's very competent. She'll be down to see you after five. She asked that you call her if you need anything. Did you find the bag she packed for you there? She included your cell phone. You'll need to check if you can use it here."

"So she's at the office…working?" His voice contained a note of surprise.

"Didn't you hire her?"

"Of course…fifteen bucks an hour…but I'm not there to show her what to do; I guess I thought she'd just shut down till I got back."

The judge chuckled. "Not Leanne. She can run that office all by herself; she's used to cranky clients…a sick boss! By the end of the month you'll be glad to pay her twenty an hour and know she's worth every cent."

He smiled as he tried to visualize a secretary worth that kind of money. *That'll be the day!* he thought.

She called on the hospital phone at 4:30. "Hello, Mr. Walker, it's Leanne. Ben tells me you're able to have visitors; okay if I come up around 5:30?"

"Well, hello. I'd be glad to have you come, and thank you for the bag you packed for me and the very lovely flower." He smiled as he glanced at the huge white lily embedded in fern and the small card that simply said, *Please…get well soon. Your Staff.* "I tried to call you this afternoon, but you seemed to be out of the office."

"Yes, indeed. I had a lot of errands. This legal business is exhausting. I'll tell you all about it when I come. I've packed your files on the three boys—some interesting developments. Anything else I should bring?"

He found himself impatient for her to arrive. He needed to know what was going on in that office, and what kind of errands could possibly keep her busy all afternoon.

He stood with his back to her, gazing out the window. Her breath caught…she had not prepared herself…the robe and slippers! He could be mistaken for her father—except for the sandy hair.

15

He turned as he heard her step. *How can she look so fresh at the end of the day?* he wondered. "Thank you again for your thoughtfulness. Tell me how you came up with all of these masculine amenities—in such record time."

"My father's," she explained.

"He didn't mind your loaning them?"

"Not at all." She smiled. "My father is gone."

"For how long?"

"About three and a half weeks."

"And he didn't take his pyjamas?"

"No," she replied. "They have no night there."

He stopped for a moment, then flushed. "I'm sorry…so very sorry…I'm sure I must have heard about your father's passing; it just didn't register. How terribly clumsy of me!"

"Not at all," she replied, opening her bulging briefcase.

"I'm sure you won't want to look at these tonight," she offered, "but there are a few things I thought you might want to contemplate tomorrow." She turned to the references and materials she had gathered from teachers and coaches over the last two days.

He glanced at the statement from Reverend Bill Somerville regarding Gregg Romero and she noticed a look of cynicism cross his handsome face. "Looks like a winner," he commented.

"Oh, yes, Jerry Coombs' father was in…wanting to see you. I told him you wouldn't be in the office for a few days but that you would need a retainer if you are going to represent Jerry. I asked for five grand. Is that okay?" She looked at him, shrugging her shoulders slightly.

He nodded as she continued, "And Janet Dewalt was in. Have you met her?"

"Yes, I have…a single mom…Dan's mother. I met her at the jail the night the boys were picked up. Why do you ask?"

"She was…rather demanding…determined. I asked for a retainer. She was indignant…said she would deal with you personally. I told her she would not deal with you at all without a check forthcoming. She finally gave me a check for the five grand, but warned me not to deposit it for a few days while she arranges for the money."

"Wow, you've put in a full week in just two days. Ever considered going into law?"

"It has crossed my mind a time or two," she replied off-handedly as she continued to bring forth press releases and explanations.

Suddenly, he found himself resenting her. *So who does she think she is, taking over my office, my investigation, my practice—my life? And what does she get out of this? Her salary doubled? Everything has its price!*

She noticed an edge to his voice when he spoke, "Well, I guess if I stay in here a few more days you'll have the office running like a top...the trial underway...."

He stopped at the look of dismay that crossed her face. "Oh, Mr. Walker...I am sorry. I didn't mean to give the impression... " she paused, "but you did hire me to be your executive assistant. I didn't know...I guess...maybe what I need is a job description."

"Perhaps we'd better work on that."

"Can we do that now?" She shuffled the papers in her briefcase and found a note pad. "What would you like me to do tomorrow? Or would you rather I closed the office until you're back?"

She was taking charge again. It infuriated him. "So...what's this about? You want a raise?"

Her face showed that his remark had struck home. "Mr. Walker," she said softly, "you are cruel." In a moment she had gathered her briefcase and small handbag, and was gone.

He sat where she had left him...the files stacked neatly for his perusal. *Nice work, Walker! You've sure done it this time! What gets into you? Why can't you just accept that you need this girl?* He rose to his feet. His eye caught sight of the shapely lily. *It's like her,* he thought. One minute he wanted to smash it into the waste can...the next he wanted to touch his lips to its gentle loveliness. He didn't understand himself.

He stretched out on the bed and lay thinking. Why did she so get under his skin? Was it just that he needed a good assistant?...or was it that he wanted it to be her? It couldn't be, he decided. He'd always been happy as a bachelor. Women! Always an ulterior motive! Still...he needed to apologize. She had done nothing worthy of his insolence. He would order flowers in the morning. A whole dozen white lilies, and he would beg her forbearance. Where would he send them? To her home address? He wasn't sure where she lived—Elmwood? Elmdale? Elm...something or other. He could send them to the office, of course...but would she be there after this? Then an idea struck him. He rose quickly and checked the inside pocket of his sport jacket. Yes...his day minder was there. Her phone number was in it. He would call her at home if she didn't answer at the office in the morning.

He slept fitfully. The dream had come back again...haunting...suffocating...terrifying! He wakened early and fought to put the bitter thoughts behind him. He tried to concentrate on what he would say to Leanne. By eight o'clock he had mentally rehearsed his lines a hundred times. Still, he was relieved to hear the beep...beep that told him the phone was busy. He hung up. She was there! She was in the office! He hastened to order the flowers. His message was brief. *Please forgive. I appreciate you more than you know. Brett.*

Why am I acting like a teenager? he asked himself, his heart hammering. He would not be disappointed if she didn't come after five today; after all, she usually had a class on Thursday evenings. The jangling of the phone broke his reverie. "Good morning," he spoke cheerfully, then found it hard to hide his disappointment when the judge answered. Would he like him to drop in this afternoon?

A perusal of the files she had brought left him speechless. She not only read and understood each situation, but had acted with knowledge and understanding. What kind of an assistant would know such things? She was like a lawyer. Letters were all ready for his signature.

He broached the subject with Judge Ben in the afternoon.

"A lawyer? Yes, indeed!" The judge chuckled. "She doesn't have a whole lot of course work left...probably less than a year...and she'll be ready to article. She reduced her classes to two nights a week to care for her dad after the accident. She was determined that her brother should finish since he was farther along than she. He will be articling this year. I think she plans to work for a time before she goes back to U of T. She seems to be questioning whether she still wants to pursue law...." He paused at the look of astonishment on Brett's face.

"No wonder," he muttered. "No jolly wonder!"

CHAPTER THREE

It's eight o'clock. What is the light doing on in my office? he wondered as the cab swished up to the rain-drenched building. The judge had offered a ride from the hospital but he hated to call when his release had not come till 7:30 in the evening. He would just drop up and see, since his car was still in the parking lot. It grated on him that she had not called since her visit on Wednesday evening, nor had she been in on Friday morning when he called the office. Voice mail told him she would be in at 1:00 p.m. and invited him to leave a number. Indignant, he had not done so.

"WHAT are you doing in my office at this hour?"

His voice startled her. She had been so absorbed that she had not heard him enter.

"Oh," she said, struggling to regain her composure, "Mr. Mancini needed to have his last Will and Testament redrawn before he leaves for Europe on Monday. My computer quit or I would have finished it by closing time. I wasn't able to do it this morning, since I had a final exam…so I thought I would just finish it before I leave. I'm sorry to have invaded your private space; I just thought…that you would rather I use your computer than take it home…out of the office." She paused, realizing she was stammering. "Perhaps I can finish it Monday morning," she offered as she quickly backed up her document and closed down his computer.

He stood watching her…not sure where to go from here. He had obviously blown it again. Why did his temper always get the best of

19

him…just when he most needed to be civil? He needed to say something…fast…she would be gone in seconds.

"Leanne, I'm sorry…again! I didn't mean that to sound like a rebuke…honest…I am impressed…." He broke off, realizing she wasn't listening but was quickly gathering her jacket and briefcase. "Have you had supper?" he asked in a last-ditch effort to stall her.

"No…thought I'd be finished…."

She was almost at the door. "Can I buy you supper?"

"That won't be necessary," she replied as the door closed behind her.

"Drats," he muttered to himself. "Walker, you are a jackass!"

He paused on the doorstep, trying to discern whether the soloist was on CD.

"A religious assistant," he muttered as he heard the words of a familiar hymn. "Just what I need!" Then feeling like a peeping tom, he rang the bell.

The music stopped abruptly and she scurried to open the door. "You're early. I wasn't expecting…why Mr. Walker! Whatever are you doing out there in the rain? You should be in bed."

"Please let me in; I'd like to make amends for my clumsiness. I hope you like pizza," he offered her the box of steaming cheese and pepperoni.

"Yes…yes…of course. Come in. Could you use a coffee while I towel my hair?" She indicated the towel twisted around her freshly showered hair. "Does the pizza need to stay warm for a few minutes? Actually I have a pot of soup on."

He noticed the table set for two and the full pot of coffee. *She was obviously expecting somebody else; small wonder she's so disappointed!*

He sipped his coffee slowly as he gazed around the kitchen. It was creatively done—the latest in expensive appliances…curtains in warm earth tones harmonizing with the oak cabinets… everything clean and in order.

He could smell a wood fire somewhere, but she had waved him to the breakfast nook in the kitchen. He dared not investigate; he had blown it enough for one short week.

"I'm sorry, I seem to be interrupting your evening," he began as she joined him.

"Not at all. Why would you think that?"

"I gather you were expecting someone?"

"Yes, I am. Dave comes home on Friday evenings. I was a little surprised to hear the doorbell; he doesn't usually arrive till after nine."

"Dave?"

"Yes. He's finishing his LLB in Toronto...comes home for the weekends."

"So...you live together?"

"Just on the weekend."

"He comes to see you every weekend?"

"Just the last month or so. Though he doesn't really come to see me; he comes to see Sherry."

"And this is okay with you?" he asked, trying to make sense out of what seemed total chaos.

"Why wouldn't it be? We both grew up with Sherry; she's a super gal." She stopped suddenly at the look on his face. "What seems to be troubling you, Mr. Walker?"

"You share your boyfriend with a girlfriend?"

"Oh...no.... Sorry! Guess I thought you knew Dave; he's my brother. We've been trying to work through some things with Dad's estate."

He shook his head as though unable to believe his own stupidity.

"Dave seems to know you. Said you instructed a couple of his classes a year or two ago."

"Dave...Stevenson," he mused. "Is he tall...dark curly hair...top-of-the-class kind of guy?"

"Sounds like Dave."

"Then I guess I do know him." He sat silently as though struggling to remember, then slowly, "His mom and dad were in an accident...your mom and dad...your dad was Bertrand Stevenson...the lawyer…who went to court in his wheel chair…and forgave the boys who caused the accident…that killed his wife?"

She nodded.

"Sorry for not getting it together sooner. I should have seen the resemblance to Dave…recognized the name…something! Guess I've just been too preoccupied. Forgive me!"

"Nothing to forgive. You've just had way too much on your plate."

"Can you tell me what happened this evening in the office…why you were offended?"

"I wasn't offended, Mr. Walker."

"Can't you call me Brett?"

"Of course, Mr. Walker…Brett. Guess I felt I had invaded your privacy…your professional boundaries…you seem so protective…."

"Protective of what?"

"Well, the other night at the hospital I got the impression that I had stepped way over the line…that I was taking over your practice. You think I have an ulterior motive. When you saw me at your computer…what went through your mind? Did you think I was attempting to gain privileged information of some sort? I don't know whether my self esteem has ever been so battered in one short week."

He continued to look at her, his face somewhat flushed. When he did not respond, she continued, "I want to assure you, Mr. Walker, that I have no designs on you, your practice, your money, or anything else. You asked for help; I thought that's what I was providing. It would seem to me to be the better part of wisdom for us to discontinue…."

"Hold it! Right there! I know we've gotten off to a bad start; I take responsibility…totally! I've been uptight and ill-tempered; I haven't apologized this often in my entire lifetime…but please…one more chance?"

She opened her mouth as if to reply, then closed it.

"Please," he reiterated.

She sighed. "I don't know, Brett. I had planned to come in on Monday morning and finish the Will that I promised to Mr. Mancini. That's the only commitment I have at the office. After that I…I really think it would be best…."

"You really did say you'd help me for at least a few weeks, you know. Can you…will you give me one more try?"

She hesitated, then smiled. "Maybe I do want something from you, after all."

He looked at her questioningly.

"Lay down the hatchet."

"It's a deal. If you'll promise not to run away again. Really, Leanne, I can't have you charging out of the office…." They both chuckled. "Agreed?"

"Agreed."

"Hi, Lee, I'm home."

"Sounds like big brother. He'll be glad to see you again."

"Well, hello, there, Mr. Walker. Remember me?" His greeting was warm and genuine as he extended his hand.

"I do…yes…a top student as I recall?"

"Hardly…but thanks for thinking well of me."

"I see by the smile…and by the clock…you've already stopped in the next block," his sister noted.

"Nope. Haven't seen her yet; the rain slowed me up. I talked to her on the cell. We'll spend most of tomorrow together…got a few plans to discuss."

"I just bet you have," she responded as they exchanged warm smiles.

"So we've taken to entertaining in the kitchen?" Dave looked at his sister.

"Why not?" She shrugged.

"Actually, I just dropped by. Leanne wasn't expecting me. I spent the week in hospital with flu and Leanne was good enough to keep the office going…." He broke off, realizing he wasn't really answering the question.

"I have some soup, and Brett brought pizza," she offered.

"Ah, nothing like home. I wasn't cut out to be a bachelor; I'd sure have to brush up on it if I had to survive long term."

"That doesn't seem likely to happen." She smiled.

"Sounds like something in the offing?" Brett questioned..

The younger man smiled warmly. "Sometime this summer, the Lord willing. Got to get this schooling out of the way."

"Where will you article? Has that been decided?"

"Hencken, Hencken and Mears in Toronto have made a rather tempting offer. Problem is that Sherry's teaching job is in London. I've done about enough running back an' forth these last few years…and I'll be learning to be a husband…so, I've been stalling…trying to make up my mind; it would certainly be a good opportunity…renowned, established firm…not bad money."

"Is that the only reason you're hesitating?"

"Well, there is the fact that they have so many lawyers in the firm. Chances at actual court time would be nil. I've talked to some of the guys there; they're pretty disappointed; most of them turn out to be gophers."

"If you decide not to go that route, I'd be glad to have you article with me. I'm pretty overwhelmed most of the time…could use a good man…lots of opportunity to be involved in all kinds of law. I have the office space…we could discuss salary…."

A low whistle. "Wow! Wow! Sounds like an offer that should be explored."

"I'll be in the office most of tomorrow," he said as he rose to go. "Give me a call."

"What do you think, Lee?" he asked as the door closed behind the lawyer.

"*Overwhelmed* is a good word to describe what's going on in his practice…but I'm not sure he's a team player, Dave. He realizes he needs help, but he resents me. I can't explain it; he seems so angry inside, always ready to lash out…attack. What can I say? He's a very popular lawyer, obviously has more clients than he can handle. If you could get along with him, it would be super. You'd get to stay in London…lots of work…lots of opportunity for court work. We need to pray about this. And you'll need to discuss it with Sherry—even before you talk to him."

He nodded as she continued. "I haven't really gotten to know him this week. He's been in hospital since Tuesday…just got out before he came here. He's sure not like Dad; he's suspicious…always thinks I have an ulterior motive. I told him I would help him for a few weeks until he finds somebody else."

"Really, Lee? You're not planning to stay?"

"I'm taking my big brother's advice very seriously. Don't think I want to commit to full-time with somebody like him."

CHAPTER FOUR

"I hoped you'd be standing by," she remarked as he answered his cell phone. "I wondered if you knew that the power outage has affected your office building."

"No, I didn't know. I don't have any power at my place, but I'm not sure why."

"Lightning hit one of the main transformers sometime after midnight Sunday; they'll be working on it most of the day." He muttered something under his breath as she continued, "You are welcome to work at my place."

"What about the law library?"

"Sorry, all that section is out. We have Dad's library here; it may have what you're looking for."

"Let me think on it. I'll need a shower…shave…breakfast."

"You can do that here…if you're comfortable, I mean. No extra charge," she quipped.

"So what time would suit you?"

"Whenever you're ready."

He smelled bacon and coffee as she opened the door. *No wonder Dave likes to come home on weekends. I'd come, too, if….* He hadn't allowed himself to think that before, and hurried to follow directions to Dave's bedroom and shower. Clean towels…soap…shampoo…. *A guy could really get into this kind o' thing!*

❦

"This is mighty fine! Do you always eat this much for breakfast?" he asked as they sat in the breakfast nook enjoying orange slices, poached eggs, bacon, toast and coffee.

"No. I only make bacon and eggs when Dave's home, but I always make sure I have an adequate breakfast. Morning is my most productive time, so I like to be ready to meet the day. Do I take it you don't care for…?"

"No, no, that's not it at all. Sometimes I just don't feel like making it…sometimes I stop at Tim Horton's—not the best idea—and sometimes I just let it go. I must say I appreciate your taking me in today; this is really special. Thank you for being so gracious."

"I'll show you the library," she suggested as they finished, and she replenished his coffee. "You should find most of what you need." She led him through the family room to the huge sliding doors that gave way to the library. A massive oak desk dominated one end of the room, backed by two walls of ceiling-to-floor volumes. At the other end, the wood-fired hearth crackled happily. He guessed there was a view of the backyard from the picture window…when the weather wasn't using it as a water slide. The two computers caught his eye. Leanne and her father had probably worked side by side during his last year.

As if she read his thoughts, she explained, "When Dad became too weak to go to the office, we just moved him in here, and we worked together. He wound up a lot of loose ends in his final year; that pleased him. He couldn't have died happy with so many things left hanging."

"This must be really handy for Dave when he comes."

"For both of us. We've benefited a great deal from having Dad at home this past year—his experience…his expertise…his advice…his library. In many ways he's still with us; he left a rich heritage!"

"Looks like I'm in the right place to do my research. *Family law…young offenders*," he read as he checked the shelves. "Were you planning to work with me today?"

"Whatever your pleasure. I had intended to be at the office. I've finished Mr. Mancini's Will. Shall I call and have him come? He wants to fly this afternoon?"

"By all means…please…if you don't mind his coming here."

She hastened to make the arrangements and in due time a smiling Mr. Mancini was on his way to Europe, satisfied that his personal affairs were in order.

"So how is your day going?" she asked as they sat by the fire, sharing soup and sandwiches.

"Great. I must say I'm impressed with your library…among other things. I can hardly believe how much I'm enjoying the day, considering how it started out. Thank you again for accommodating me."

"I'm enjoying it, too. Glad we didn't have to waste the day."

"How would you feel if Dave came to article with me? Would that make a difference in whether you stay?"

She stiffened slightly. "Which question do you want answered first?"

"The one about Dave."

She toyed with her spoon, glancing up at him a time or two. "Mr. Walker…Brett, I'm not sure it's the best idea."

"Why is that? Am I really that bad; first *you* can't work with me…now Dave?"

Ignoring his question, she went on. "Dave is a lot like me—he's a mover and a shaker. He's also kind, caring, accommodating. I think you would have the same problem with him that you do with me…you would think that…. I would have a hard time…."

"You don't think Dave can look out for himself?"

"Should he have to? If he's on your team?"

"So? Will you discourage him from articling with me?"

"No. No, of course not."

"But you won't stay…even if Dave comes on board?"

"I don't know. I really don't know. Dave and I have always been close…more so since we lost Mom and Dad.. Wouldn't it only be a matter of time before you felt ganged up on? And…I need to get on with my education…finish my LLB; half a degree isn't worth a lot.

Dave would like to see me return to U of T for my final year, and graduate next spring. I plan to do that, whether or not I decide to stay with law."

"And if you don't work in law, what are you thinking?"

"Possibly investigative journalism. I really don't know at this point."

"How does Dave feel about that?"

"Not good…but I really can't live my life by how Dave feels."

"So, why do you not want to be a lawyer?"

"Not sure. Not sure that I don't—just no longer sure that I do."

"Did the judge think your working for me might spark something?"

"Probably. He's pretty concerned about me right now. Thinks I've lost my way."

"Have you?"

"What do you think?"

"I think you're already a very gifted lawyer. I would jump at the chance to have you on my team one day…." *In more ways than one*, he mused.

"Thanks for the vote of confidence."

"So, have you discussed his articling?"

"Very briefly…before he met with you. I understand you'll be getting together again next weekend?"

"Actually, I'm expecting Dave and Sherry to come for a barbeque on Saturday night. Guess I was hoping you'd join us. It will be good to meet Sherry…give us some time to discuss questions and details. Will you come?"

For a moment he thought she would refuse, then she nodded as she rose to clear the table. "Would you mind if I called Reverend Somerville and asked him to stop by? I'd like him to explain some of the statements he's made here."

"Please feel free. Dad's clients often came. They used the side door to keep it a little more professional."

CHAPTER FIVE

"Will you join us, Lee?" he asked as she showed Bill Somerville into the library.

"Now, Mr. Somerville…may I call you Bill? Your statement is pretty clear that you believe the Romero boy to be totally innocent. I get the impression that you will accept nothing less."

"You have interpreted that correctly."

"At this point, I have no grounds for such a belief. I have twice visited this boy and he simply refuses to co-operate…won't answer my questions…won't give me a statement. I've tried to convince him that I'm not the judge and jury; I'm his defense…his advocate…his chance at acquittal. Does he realize that he is accused of second-degree murder?…that of the three, he is the one most likely to get a lengthy sentence?"

"Hold on! Just hold on a minute, there!" Lee was surprised at the intensity of the young pastor's voice. "Not only do I know Gregg…know him well…but I know his whole family. Believe me, there is no possibility…."

"That won't cut it, Reverend. The boy was standing over the victim with a dripping knife in his hand when the police arrived. The other two were running…had no weapons of any kind. It would seem that of the three…."

"My statement clearly sets out that Gregg was on his way home from church; he had been helping with a children's club. He was on his bike. What if he took a shortcut through the alley…heard the guard's cry for help and stopped…saw the man lying there and tried to help…thought he should pull out the knife…then the police arrived?"

"He wouldn't talk to them, either. His silence can only be interpreted as guilt."

"Or fear…or shock," Lee cut in, as her pastor nodded.

"He was in total shock when his parents and I were called to the police station the night of the killing. He couldn't speak. I think the incident in the alley was enough to render him speechless…never mind being charged with murder," he added.

"Lee, are you familiar with this family?"

"Yes, certainly. I don't know them nearly as well as Pastor Somerville does. I know Gregg somewhat…always busy helping…working with kids. A nice, clean-cut kind of boy. Statements from the school bear out that he's the same at school…good marks…on the swim team…a good attitude toward authority. I can't for the life of me see him involved in breaking and entering…far less getting involved in this bank-card scam."

"So…do the two of you think that Gregg might talk to Leanne…give her a statement that we could make sense of?"

"Leanne would be far less threatening," the pastor suggested. "Gregg and his parents see her as an ally in a world suddenly gone awry. I think he would do his best to co-operate."

"Leanne, are you willing?" She nodded. "Good, can we head down there within the hour?"

"I'm sorry. I have an appointment at 5:15 on Mondays…until 7:00."

"This is more important than Gregg's life, Leanne?" her pastor questioned.

"Of equal importance. I have a commitment to Brody and his mom on Monday nights."

The pastor nodded understandingly.

"Fine, we'll go first thing in the morning. I'll visit Dan and Jerry while you call on Gregg. We'll need some pretty compelling evidence to keep this out of the adult arena. The crime is murder…these kids could get a lot of years in a detention center."

"Gregg is innocent, Mr. Walker," the pastor reminded him.

"You religious people make me laugh. You seem to think that once a person has *got religion* he can pre-empt justice. Do you realize what the press would do with a story like that? Public opinion is against us; we can hardly cite religion as a proof of innocence."

"I'm sorry; I must take issue with that statement." The pastor's tone was conciliatory. The lawyer nodded as he continued, "In the first place, we are not religious—we are Christian."

"Aren't we splitting straws here? There's a difference?"

"Definitely. Religion is man-made. Man's attempt to find God, by his own efforts. Christianity is God-made; God's answer to man's sin problem, His way for us to come to Him…."

"Okay…okay already. You haven't addressed my point."

"I can't deny that people have tried to use religion to pre-empt justice. In Gregg's case, I believe the truth will prevail. He hardly had time to get from the church to that alley, never mind take part in a break-in and murder. What could he possibly have gotten out of it? He left the church on his bike at 9:00 p.m. and was picked up at 9:20…."

"Are there witnesses who saw him still at the church at 9:00?"

"Most of the parents who came to pick up their children from club would have seen him helping the children get their stuff together."

"We'll need names of those who saw him who will be willing to say so."

"Thanks," the pastor said as he rose to go. "Will you want me along tomorrow?"

They both looked at Leanne.

"Why not? Why don't you come with me? You know Gregg so much better than I do, and he may be more comfortable with you there."

"He's quite a guy, isn't he?" Brett remarked as Bill Somerville took his leave. "I'd like to get to know him better."

"Sorry, I've gotta run. Brody will be looking for me. Are you working till seven? Will you join me for supper?"

"Well, thank you, but you've already been so kind. Let me take you to supper?"

32

"Actually, it's in the oven. It'll be ready by the time I get back. Feel free to watch the six o'clock news. It would be good to know if the power is back on."

"Thanks, I'll do that. Guess my car is in your way," he said as he got up.

"Not really; I'm going to walk. It's only two blocks and we're between raindrops."

"Give me the house number; if we have a deluge I'll pick you up."

"Seven eleven." She laughed. "Don't worry about me, though. I've been wet a few times."

He noticed that she tucked a small casserole into her carry-all bag, and took it with her.

The doorbell rang as she finished her lesson with Brody. There had indeed been a deluge, and she was pleased to see that Brett had come for her.

"Thank you for rescuing me; I would surely have drowned. Come, meet Brody; I've been telling him about you."

He shook the water from his jacket and stepped inside. He was taken aback as he saw the small emaciated body in the wheelchair. His hands seemed tethered to small straps to keep them from floating around; his neck braced to keep his head from lolling. He attempted a smile and a garbled greeting as Lee introduced them. Then turning to his computer with the oversize keyboard, he patiently typed out, "*Hello.*"

"'Hello' to you, too," Brett managed. "That's quite the computer you have there. I bet it can do most anything?"

Again the small hands patiently forced the fingers to find the right keys. "Only if I give it a hand!"

They chuckled at his little joke.

"So…you spend every Monday night with this boy?" he asked as they pulled away from the curb. She nodded. "Tell me about him…tell me why you do this."

33

"Brody was born with cerebral palsy. When they found out, his father deserted the family; that's twelve years ago now. Melva, his mom, couldn't cope alone, so the church formed a support group for her so she could go to school. She graduated in computer science and has a small business at home. We were able to raise funds for Brody's computer. It's pretty specialized, but it means he can connect with those around him, and with the world. Makes him feel human, rather than other."

She had noticed the tightening in Brett's jaw when he saw Brody, and wondered at his reaction. Now she flinched as he asked, "So why do you do this? I gather that you see your time there as worthwhile?"

She sat quietly while they waited in the car for a break in the downpour. How could she explain to him how precious Brody was to her...to God? Finally she managed, "I have learned a great deal from Brody and from my association with him. Yes, I see it as worthwhile...even if he doesn't live very long. None of us thought he would be with us this long; he has a terrible heart problem, but I see it as worthwhile...very worthwhile! My mom used to look after Brody on Mondays when Melva was in school. She would take meals and spend the day bathing him, teaching him to read, cleaning house...anything that would take some of the weight off his mother. I would often go there after school and entertain him for a couple of hours. He's really like a little brother. Of course, I can't go that often now, and his mother is there most of the time, but I still go Monday nights and take supper. I guess...I guess if I really had to give a reason for my going, I would have to say that the love of Christ compels me."

"Yes...yes...it would have to be something like that," he said thoughtfully. "You're quite a girl, Lee! Is that why you stayed to help me...the love of Christ compelled you...?"

"Come quickly," she said opening the car door, "while the rain has let up."

CHAPTER SIX

She watched his face as he perused the statement she had taken from Gregg Romero. "Well, I'll be! The little rascal! Why didn't he tell me all this stuff?"

"Probably way too frightened; you're a scary guy." She laughed. He raised an eyebrow at her as she continued, "What do you make of the big guy that he mentions?"

"Sounds like a good alibi, if he can get away with it. Always good to blame it on somebody who isn't there."

"Come on, Brett…we're defense…not prosecution."

"Wow! Just a minute here! He says the guy yelled at the two boys, 'Wait up…it's Laser.' Jerry and Dan didn't mention any third party. Sounds like they knew this guy, Laser. Do you think this statement is credible?"

"Yeah, I do. He said the man was heavy set…described him as running rather clumsily…had an accent…maybe a Latino of some sort."

She noticed his facial muscles tighten and his voice took on that familiar edge. "I knew a guy like that once…called himself *Radar*…used younger boys to do his dirty work…let them take the rap while he walked away unscathed."

"Maybe we have the same guy with a name change," she ventured, watching anger smolder in his dark eyes. *This is more personal than he's letting on*, she thought. *I wonder if he was one of the boys….*

"I'm back to the jail to confront my two guys with this. If I get a statement from them to this effect, I'm going to the police."

She was still deeply absorbed in thought, when Janet Dewalt burst through the door.

"Brett is expecting me," she announced as she sailed toward his office.

"I'm sorry Mr. Walker is not in; you really should make an appointment if you wish to see him; he's a very busy man. Lee found herself resenting the provocative dress…the too-familiar manner…calling him *Brett*. She was suddenly glad he was not in.

Janet was indignant. "He knew I'd be coming today. He's defending my son; it's high time he got him out of there. He knows he's not guilty. So where can I find him?"

"Here…this afternoon…if you have an appointment. Shall we say three o'clock?"

"How dare he keep me waiting this way!" She flounced out of the office, much to Lee's relief.

Thank you, God, she muttered. *Thank you that she didn't sit down to wait.*

"Join me for a few minutes," he said as he came through the door.

"I was about to have a sandwich. Want to share half 'n' half—BLT and corned beef?"

"Sounds good to me. I'm starved."

She poured them each a coffee as he began, "Have I had an interesting morning, or what? Those boys are positive rascals…scared rascals. Faced with Gregg's statement, they finally admitted that there was a third party to their crime. They don't know Gregg…never saw him…didn't know there had been a murder until the police caught up to them. They hardly know this *Laser*…said he started hanging around the soccer field. They thought he was some kind of a coach at first. He talked to them a few times, then asked them if they would like to make some easy money. They were interested. All they had to do was to give him their parents' bank card and make sure they knew the pin number. They would each get a bonus of $200.00. There would be no loss to the parents, he assured them."

"So, he used their parents' accounts in some way?"

"Right. The idea was to enter the store after hours and use the card to effect refunds…which would be deposited to the account. From there…a simple matter to stop at a cash machine and collect."

"Pretty slick. But why were the boys involved in the actual operation?"

"First I understand, they were intrigued with the easy money. Then they became frightened and backed off. He was ready for them…told them the money came from a biker gang and they couldn't play games with them. They tried to give the money back; of course, he refused. It was a hoax but he had them so frightened they wouldn't tell…even in the face of a murder charge."

"Well, I'll be!"

"I went to the police and they filled me in. This *Radar* just got out of jail a couple months ago. His modus operandi is to have the boys do the dirty work. They don't think the $200.00 each came from a break-in…probably from his mother. He doesn't go in himself anymore…security cameras…he's too well known. Detective Goetz came back to the cells with me and we took statements from each of the boys separately. Each didn't know the other had talked. They both told the same story. This *Laser* had made friends with a third boy on the soccer team; he works in the sporting-goods store after school and on Saturdays, sort of a security person; guess they'll be picking him up after school. He was recruited to ensure that the alarm wouldn't cut in until after 11:00 p.m. Store closed at 8:00 on week nights."

"Wow! Pretty cool! They didn't lose any time getting in and getting the job done. Do you know who the other boy is?"

"Name is Rob Chambers; his dad is Bert Chambers."

"Why does that sound familiar…Bert Chambers?"

"He owns the sporting-goods store."

She sat stunned, then managed a small, "Oh!"

"It would have been quite lucrative if the night watchman hadn't come along. When he noticed somebody inside, he put in a call to the police. Then he watched for the boys to come out. Unfortunately, he wasn't the only one watching for the boys to come out—Laser was lurking in the shadows."

"For?"

"Probably intended to take the bank cards from the boys by force if they didn't surrender them peaceably; why else the knife? The guard must have come upon him unexpectedly and there was a scuffle...the knife was handy."

"The wretch! And the police think this *Laser* is *Radar* with a name change?"

"They're pretty sure...operates the same way. The boys described him the same way that Gregg did. Seems little doubt. He's a *Latino*."

"The way you say that word scares me. Do you have something against people of that descent?" she asked, noticing his eyes were dark with anger.

"I'll tell you a little story one day...."

"Sounds like Mrs. Dewalt has arrived an hour early; I told her 3:00."

"Show her in; may as well get on with it."

No need to show her in. Leanne grimaced as Janet floated past her and into the lawyer's office. She noted that the harsh, commanding tone used on her had now turned soft and seductive. "Brett...at long last," she purred as Lee pulled the door shut behind her.

"Really, Brett," she continued, "you really must do something about that secretary of yours. Honestly! She is quite impossible!"

"In what way?"

"I've been trying to see you for days; she simply refuses to allow me...she really is...."

"I've been away. But it's essential that she guard my time...she's very careful and efficient in what she does."

"I suppose those kind are necessary! Oh, well...on to more important matters."

"I saw your son this morning, Mrs. Dewalt."

"Janet."

"As you wish...Janet."

"I want him out of there, Brett; you know he's not guilty. He couldn't possibly be involved in such a thing. I know him...I raised him myself."

"Mrs. Dewalt...."

"Janet."

"Very well, Janet. Are you telling me that your bank card is not missing?"

Quickly she opened her purse and deposited the card on his desk.

"This is a replacement card, is it not?"

"Why would you say such a thing? Are you accusing me of…?"

"Yes, Janet. The police have your original card and your son has confessed to stealing it and using it in the store."

"Don't be ridiculous. He's being framed…we're being framed. I thought you were our lawyer. What are you going to do about this?"

"Perhaps we could begin with your giving me an honest statement, Mrs. Dewalt," he suggested as he buzzed for Leanne. "Could you come in, please, Lee. Mrs. Dewalt would like to give us a statement."

She rose haughtily as Leanne entered. "Well, I never…." Her eyes blazed, as her colour heightened. "How dare you treat me like a common…!"

"Sit down, please, Mrs. Dewalt. Your son is in prison; he is accused of second-degree murder. I appreciate your going to bat for him…but to deny what we already have proof of is not the way to go. It can only discredit you both."

"I'm sorry…sorry that I have allowed you to represent us. Consider yourself fired!"

"Actually, Mrs. Dewalt, I haven't as yet been hired. Your check is being held…waiting for funds. When you have thought this thing over, you may want to come back and we'll do business. Your son has the potential to go either way at this stage. I suggest you give him a fighting chance…an example that he can be proud of."

She sat on the edge of her chair…shame slowly creeping up her neck and showing through her heavy makeup. "Fine," she said; then rising quickly as though her mind was made up, she added, "I'll be in touch."

They sat looking at each other. "You don't like her, do you?" he asked.

"Not especially."

"Why is that?"

"I react to her pushiness…I'll get what I want when I want. Then her dress…always so seductive. I guess I feel…I think…." She stopped.

"Go on."

"No."

"Yes."

"Fine. I guess I think she intended to pay the $5,000…in some way…other than cash."

He was amused now. "What way?"

"You figure it out…you're the lawyer."

His laughter was refreshing. "And you set me up with this bombshell? Knowing what she was about to propose?"

"I didn't know…I thought…because she said she would deal with you personally concerning the financing…with a 'you'd never understand' look in her eye…."

"I thought you might have tried to protect me…."

"You seem to do pretty well on your own. Guess I thought you could handle it. You proved me right."

He looked amused as she filled his coffee cup and headed back to her computer.

"Rascal!" she muttered to herself.

"I want to see the lawyer," the man snarled as he came through the door.

"Why, yes sir…certainly. I take it you don't have an appointment. May I tell him your name?"

"Chambers," he growled impatiently.

"Come right this way, sir," she said as she replaced the phone. "Mr. Walker will see you now."

"You bet he will," he muttered as he brushed past her.

They're having an awful time in there, she thought as voices rose and fell. *Sure hope he doesn't get violent.* At length the older man emerged, dishevelled and perspiring, but seemingly placated.

"Give Mr. Chambers a receipt for five thousand dollars," the lawyer directed as he returned to his office.

This lawyer is something else, she mused. *How many men do I know that can take on a wild man…tame him…and wind up with five grand?*

Her intercom buzzed. "Will you come in, Lee?"

She sat looking at him across the desk. "Honestly, Brett. I was ready to call 9-1-1."

"Not to worry. He was distraught…his only son…involved in robbing him…refused to believe it was true. Blamed me for getting the other two boys to implicate him. Even suggested that I was looking for greater press coverage…higher profile…to say nothing of lining my pockets. I told him I would take responsibility for finding out the truth. Suggested he'd be better off looking for a motive than trying to deny the whole thing. Poor man…he's in shock."

CHAPTER SEVEN

"What a gorgeous evening for a barbeque," Sherry noted as she relaxed on the patio, her blonde hair draped gracefully over her shoulders. "I thought that rain would just never stop."

Leanne enjoyed chit-chatting with her friend and watching Dave at the barbeque, while Brett finished the Caesar salad. *He's incredibly handsome*, she thought as she watched him put the finishing touches on the table. She had never seen him so relaxed...enjoying himself...his polo shirt open at the neck...white apron covering his khakis.... *Get a grip, Lee*, she warned herself, *he's not for you.*

"Looks like we're ready here," Dave announced as he lifted the steaks onto a platter.

"Fit for a king!" Sherry complimented as they looked at the spread before them.

"Looks like you've done this a time or two," Lee suggested.

Brett smiled and nodded at Dave to ask the blessing.

As the supper wound down and coffees were refilled and carried out to the patio, it became apparent that the men were seeing eye to eye on the articling decision. Sherry was totally taken with Brett and delighted to think that she and Dave might actually live together the first year of their marriage. Lee watched without comment...happy for all of them...feeling more and more comfortable with Dave and Brett working together.

"Sorry, we'll need to go," Dave remembered as the clock chimed *nine.* "We promised Sherry's mom...."

"Please feel free. I've probably kept you longer than I should. Thanks for coming. Glad to meet you, Sherry, and...Dave...hey...I can't tell you how glad I am to have you on board!"

"Me, too," Dave agreed.

"And me," from Sherry. "But Dave, we should be helping...."

"Leave that for me," Leanne chimed in. "I'm not in a rush...and I already know how to wash his coffee mugs."

"Thanks, Lee, for coming...and for staying. Are you more comfortable with Dave working with me?"

"Yes. Yes, I am. I think you'll really enjoy each other."

"What made you change your mind?"

"I guess this past week...I've seen a different side of you."

"Really? Does that mean I...may have a chance...that you may change your mind and stay until fall?"

She nodded rather shyly.

"Really? Has Dave's decision made a difference?"

"Possibly, but I think I made my decision after the Monday when we worked together at my place. Guess I thought if we could work together for a whole day without conflict, maybe we could do it every day."

"Wow! This has got to be the best day I've had in years!" He wondered what she would do if he grabbed her and gave her a hug. *Discretion...better part of valour*, he warned himself.

"Got time to join me for a coffee before you go?" he asked hopefully as he saw her pick up her jacket.

"Sure enough."

"Getting a bit cool on the patio," he commented as he set the tray on the small coffee table in the living room. She nodded as he continued making conversation. "Dave and Sherry tell me the date has been set for August 1. Sure one happy couple!"

"They really are. Grew up together. I think they've been in love since they were in their teens...always preferred one another over everybody else."

"She is a beautiful gal. A natural blonde?"

"Oh, yeah. Has a brother just like her—blonde and blue-eyed."

"Really? Older or younger?"

"Older. Same age as Dave. Actually, they're in the same program at U of T. They'll be graduating together."

"Sorry I didn't know, or I'd have asked him to come tonight. Is he a special friend of yours?"

"Yeah, sure, we grew up together, played together like Dave and Sherry."

"Fell in love like Dave and Sherry?" He kicked himself for being so forward, but felt he just had to know.

"Not really. Bob is a special guy. He'll be an incredible lawyer. But, he's not my type at all."

Relief flooded him as he struggled for words. "I hear there'll be a graduation party for Dave at the end of the month."

"Yes. The judge, Uncle Ben, won't have it any other way. He's so proud of Dave you'd think he was his dad. He's dear. He won't spare any expense. It will be quite gala—dining and dancing at the Ramada. I hope you're planning to come."

"Yes. Yes, I am. The judge invited me himself…then Dave mentioned it earlier this evening. I'm happy to be included; happy they…and you, would like me to be there."

"We would, indeed. See you Monday." She smiled as she rose to go.

Chapter Eight

"I'll be in juvenile court most of the morning…need to spend some time with the prosecutor," he said as he slid some files into his briefcase. "They need to let Romero out of there…they can't possibly make a case against him."

"Shall I book appointments for this afternoon?"

"Not unless it's an emergency. I'll need the time to prepare…think through…my approach on this thing. We need to keep those boys in the juvenile system. Prosecutor wants to transfer to adult court; I think he's bowing to public opinion. The press sure isn't helping. Have you seen what they've done with the Chambers kid? Some cub reporter trying to make a name for himself…makes me sick!"

She watched him go with a prayer, *O, please God…he needs all the help he can get.*

The afternoon edition said it all, *OFFENDER WITH BLOODY KNIFE FREED—CHARGES DROPPED.* The article went on to give details, citing Brett Walker as the criminal lawyer responsible for the release. His picture as he came down the courthouse steps with the prosecutor added to the strong implication—obviously a deal had been cut.

<hr/>

"Shouldn't we celebrate with supper?" he asked as she prepared to leave at five.

"It's my night with Brody."

"Lee," he said in a tone that made her hesitate, "we could go after seven!"

She hesitated so long that he continued, "I thought we had agreed to be friends. Is there something wrong with friends enjoying supper together? Would you be more comfortable if I ordered Chinese and we ate in the office?"

"Brett." She managed a smile. "You are being ridiculous, and you know it. Fine then…okay…we'll go to supper."

"So, I'll pick you up at seven?"

"Better give me a little time; I need to shower and change. Mondays are always hectic."

He had obviously showered and changed, too, when he came to call for her. He looked relaxed and comfortable in dress casuals, and he smiled warmly as he noticed her tan and navy shirt and pants. "You always look so lovely…refreshing, I guess I'd have to say."

"Look whose calling it!" She smiled.

"So you didn't want to come with me tonight," he began as the waitress left with their order. "Why do you find it so hard to like me?"

"Ouch! Ouch! You hit hard. Who says I don't like you?"

Their eyes met across the table. "On a scale of one to ten…where do I rate?"

"Probably a twelve."

"So you *like* me! Guess I just need to find the key to the drawbridge?"

"Drawbridge?"

He sat silently for a few seconds, then explained, "The drawbridge that gives others access…lets them cross the moat. It always pulls up just as I get there. I've never been able to find the key. What's wrong with me, Lee?" He reached across the small table and took her hand as he spoke.

"Brett…dear Brett." She placed her other hand on top of his and held it for a moment before she withdrew. "There is nothing wrong with you. You are a very special man."

"But?"

"But, what?"

"But why am I always left on the bank when the drawbridge goes up?"

"We are two very different people, Brett. We come at life from totally different world views."

"So it's the religion thing again? Pardon me…Christian thing?"

"You know that my faith in God…in Christ…is more important to me than life itself. It isn't just that you don't believe, Brett; it's that you're so antagonistic. Did you notice the tone in your voice when you said, *'religion…Christian thing'?* We'd destroy each other…."

"So that's the key to the drawbridge?"

"No…please…no…don't go there. That's not the way it works. That sounds like a come-on…it would make me feel…like God is on the bargaining table…like He's a means to an end. We can't use God. He tells us that we will seek Him, and find Him, when we search for Him with all our heart. It's only those who hunger for Him…."

"How do you know that I don't believe, Lee? I had a Christian mom until I was ten…and dad until I was twelve. I guess when God didn't answer any of my prayers for their recovery, I decided He either didn't give a hoot about me, or He didn't exist."

"How painful! And a pretty far-reaching decision for a twelve-year-old!"

"It was too painful to believe that He existed and didn't care about me. I was pretty successful in closing down the feelings…emotional stuff…until you came along…you and Dave."

"So what did we have to do with it?"

"I didn't know who you were at first. I could hardly believe it when I found out it was your folks who were killed by the teenage neighbour…that your dad…and you and Dave…forgave. Maybe it's the happy, vibrant zest you have for life that makes me wonder— maybe God is for real after all."

"He's real, Brett! He's very real! I am sorry to hear of the death of your parents; how absolutely devastating that must have been for you. Can I ask who raised you?"

"It's a long story…yes, and it's devastating. Eventually Dad's old friend found me and brought me home to live with them. He had been Dad's lawyer."

"Is that the reason…the influence…?"

"Partly. Maybe more than I realize."

"May I ask you something I've been wondering about?"

"Go for it."

"Is there some reason you don't seem to…?" She started again. "Well, I noticed your reacting to the Romero family…and you seemed so angry when Gregg described this Laser as being of Latin descent. Is there something there…some connection…some experience…?"

He struggled to keep his emotions under control…looked across at her several times, then down. The steaming platters of Chinese food sat between them untouched. "You're awfully perceptive…you should definitely be a lawyer…or a detective." He tried a grin. "Yes…I would have to say there are reasons…or maybe excuses…for my bad behaviour. Can we leave that for another time…when we're out to supper?"

"You're a rascal, Brett Walker."

"That's okay. You like rascals…twelve on a scale of one to ten."

She blushed. "Is that evidence to be used against me?"

"I guess I would call it fuel for hope. You want to thank God before we eat?"

She nodded, bowed her head and thanked the Lord. "It's almost eight…no wonder I'm so hungry. This is incredible food. Do you eat here often?"

"Sometimes…just when I'm way too tired to cook. Usually I like to make my own. By the way, how was Brody tonight?"

"I'm not sure…something not quite right there…seemed tired…distracted…no joking around…a bit clingy. I decided not to do computer…read to him all his favorite stories. He likes Pinocchio…identifies with the strings that help him move. He hated to see me go. I stayed a few minutes longer…he wanted me to hug him…seemed to need comfort…reassurance. I prayed with him before I left."

"Everybody needs a friend like you, Lee. Even those of us who think we're healthy."

She returned his warm smile.

CHAPTER NINE

"Good morning, Lee. You're in ear...ly. Whatever is the matter?"

She lifted her tear-stained face from her hands. "Brody," she sobbed, "he...he...died in the night. Melva just called."

"Oh Lee...Lee...Lee...baby, I am so sorry." He lifted her gently from her chair and put his arms around her. "Do you need to go? Can I take you somewhere?"

The door opened and a lawyer from down the hall popped in. "Early morning tete-a-tete?" he smirked.

"Early morning death in the family," Brett replied stonily.

"I can wait." The door closed quickly behind him.

"You just bet you can," Brett muttered.

"I guess I really should go and help Melva make arrangements. Pastor Somerville will be there...probably his wife...and maybe the neighbour."

"Would you like me to drive you?"

"No. No, I'll need my car in case I have to run some errands. Thank you, though. I appreciate your thoughtfulness. I should be back by noon."

"Take the day off, Lee. You shouldn't be working with all this on your mind...your heart. I'll manage." He continued as she gathered her things together. "Will you call me tonight and let me know how it's going, and what the arrangements will be?"

She nodded, then accepted his hug before he opened the door for her.

Brett didn't expect the church to be so full. How could one tiny, crippled little kid garner so much attention? He declined to follow the steady stream of mourners who filed past the open coffin. There were very few in the family bench. Lee sat with Brody's mom. He noticed that Lee's brother, Dave, sat among the pallbearers...and the tall blonde man...that must be Sherry's brother, Bob, and the lanky kid beside Dave...he couldn't tell for certain but he sure looked like Gregg Romero.

The funeral service was like nothing he had ever experienced. While there were tears, the over-riding theme was one of rejoicing...the goodness of God...the fact that Brody is now whole. In giving the eulogy, Lee shared how he had nicknamed himself *Pinocchio* because he needed strings to control his limbs.

As she finished her story, telling of his coming to Christ when he was eight, and of his love for the Lord, she turned and addressed the small body in the coffin. "Brody," she said, "we're going to miss you something terrible. You've been a part of our lives for twelve years. You and I have laughed, and played, and cried and prayed together...you've been my little brother. I'll never forget you. But today, I'm not crying for you, Brody; you've been freed from your strings...not touched by the Blue Fairy...but by God Himself. Today, I'm just crying for myself...because of the big, empty space you've left in my heart...because I won't get any more e-mails telling me how special I am...no more jokes on the computer. It makes my heart smile to imagine what a stir you must be causing in heaven...with wings instead of strings."

They walked slowly behind the small while coffin, Lee's arm steadying Melva, as she sobbed uncontrollably. Midway down the aisle, she glanced up...into the tearful face of Nate Barnes...the absentee father and husband. *How painful this must be for you,* she thought as her heart went out to the bereaved father.

Brett watched the procession from the back row…if only he could take Lee in his arms and let her know how much he cared. Would she even accept his comfort? Perhaps flowers might say it better.

The large pot of delicate Easter lilies arrived as she removed her jacket.

"Sure glad you're in early; got a lot of deliveries today…this Easter thing sure is something, isn't it?"

"It certainly is," Lee affirmed as she accepted the lovely flower. "And this beautiful white lily is a symbol of life…new life beyond the grave; that's what Easter is all about."

"Oh, boy…I sure didn't know that!" The delivery boy stumbled slightly in his haste to open the heavy door.

She smiled as she read the little card, "Just want you to know I care. Brett." She busied herself unwrapping the potted plant, putting on a fresh pot of coffee, warming up her computer…but her mind was preoccupied; what an interesting conversation they had with Brody's dad last evening.

Dave had left early…said something about meeting Brett for breakfast. Wonder if that means Brett will be late getting in, she pondered, even as the door opened and he greeted her with his usual smile.

"Mornin' Lee."

"Morning, Brett." She poured herself a coffee and held up his cup, offering to pour for him.

"Sure, thanks…and why don't you come in for a few minutes before the day gets away on us."

"How was breakfast?" she ventured.

"Great. That Dave is just one great guy. Can hardly wait for him to get here…guess that won't be long now…couple more weeks. What are you smiling about?"

"You. You just seem so much happier this last while. Can I ask why?"

"I'm not sure I know…except that having you and Dave on board…could hardly ask for more?"

"Depends on who you're asking. God's resources are unlimited."

"So I'm finding out. That funeral yesterday was something else. I was really moved."

"By?"

"The pastor's message, the stories that different ones told about Brody, what you had to say; the whole attitude seemed to be one of rejoicing…in spite of the sorrow. Amazing! Amazing to me that this little kid knew he was going to heaven."

"Yes. He was very secure in his relationship with Jesus. Just knew he was loved. I asked him one day, how he knew God cared for him. He painfully picked out his answer on the computer, 'because He sent so many peoples to love me.'"

"That's really special, Lee. But I have a question. Dave mentioned this morning that Brody's dad spent the night at your house…."

"Uh huh."

"And that he told you he never deserted his wife and son, but that she kicked him out of the house when he lost his job, and then she wouldn't let him come back because she was getting help from the church…and that if he came the church might not support her…and that she needed the help with her education and Brody…."

She nodded. "That's true. That's what he told us."

"So how do you respond to that? She lied to you all these years…and got all that help under false pretenses?"

"Melva and Nate got married at eighteen when they found out Brody was on the way. They were far too immature to handle marriage…never mind a child…a disabled one at that. They were both abused kids…not a good foundation for a relationship. They had both finished high school, which is amazing in itself. He got a job packing groceries, or some such…they could hardly eat, never mind pay the bills. Then he was laid off. I guess she was pretty frantic…screamed at him that he never did anything right…couldn't hold a job…couldn't even father a healthy child. He was pretty devastated. He got another job, but by then she had appealed to welfare, and to the church for help. The two got together and set up a program to help her and Brody."

"So claiming desertion got her the sympathy she needed?"

"Yes. Yes, she lied to us. But the really sad thing…other than the lie…is that we would have helped the family…all three of them. I don't doubt in a church that size there would be someone who would have given him a job. Social Services would have helped him get on with his education so he could get a diploma in something or other. And they would have been counseled for their pain. She gained by her lie…but she lost."

"But didn't she accept Christ somewhere along the way. I thought you said…."

"That's true."

"But she didn't see fit to tell the truth?"

"Guess not. I sure hadn't heard about this before."

"So what now?"

"We'll confront her…as kindly and lovingly as possible. She'll feel a lot better once her conscience is cleared. It wouldn't surprise me that she and Nate may still make a go of it…if they can forgive each other."

"Lee…you are something else. Aren't you angry at her? She used you all this time?"

"Not really. I would have done the same thing if Nate would have been there. But I hurt for her…not trusting us enough to tell the truth. Must have been awfully hard on her conscience."

"Well, I'll be," he muttered as she rose to see who had entered the front office.

"I want to see the lawyer…Brett Walker," the matronly Latin woman stated matter of factly.

"May I tell him your name?"

"I'm his mamma."

"Pardon me?" Lee asked in astonishment.

"I'm his mamma."

"May I tell him your name?"

"Mamma…Rosita Cortez Walker," she rolled the *r*'s as she spoke.

Lee hesitated. How should she handle this? Better not to use the *mamma* thing. Maybe she'd just slip into Brett's office and tell him Rosita Cortez Walker…."

He looked up in surprise as she mentioned the name. "I don't have time to see her today…or any other day. Tell her to go, please."

"Brett…Brett…my son, my son," she cried as she brushed past Lee and into his office.

Lee watched in astonishment as the chubby matron tried in vain to get close enough to hug the handsome lawyer. *Mamma, indeed!* she thought. How could you possibly have given birth to Brett Walker?

"Mrs. Cortez, I want you to leave my office at once; or I will call the police."

"How can you be so cruel to your own mamma?"

"I have no mamma, not since I was ten, and you have never been, or will ever be, related to me in any way whatsoever. Kindly go at once."

"You don't care about your poor brother. He is in jail…falsely accused…."

"I have no brother. If Tony is back in jail, he is justly accused. I must ask you again to leave before I have you removed. He picked up the phone."

"Cruel, cruel, that's what you are; you defend all the trash, but your own brother…." She sobbed as Leanne showed her to the waiting room. "You must talk some sense into him…he must help his brother."

"I am sorry, Mrs. Cortez. That's not my job. I'm sorry, but you must go at once." She opened the office door as she spoke and gently helped the weeping woman out into the hall.

"Lee, did the morning paper arrive?"

"Yes, I'm sorry; it was late this morning."

He took it quickly and spread it on her desk. "So they picked him up?"

There it was…Tony Cortez…alias Radar…alias Laser…charged with second-degree murder. And he looked just like his mamma.

"Get me an appointment with the prosecutor," he ordered as he picked up the paper and headed into his office.

Chapter Ten

"Will Dave want to pick his own furniture? He hasn't said anything and I keep forgetting to ask. I assume he has his eye on something special or he wouldn't have been so particular about the drapes."

"Special! Yes, I would say! He has all of Dad's office furniture. It's in storage. Dad left it to him. He'll probably want to move it in when he arrives at the end of the week. Course we need to get the party out of the way."

"So Dave got the furniture? And you?"

"I got all Mom's stuff...dining room furniture...china...all the girl stuff."

He smiled. "So what will you do with all this when you go back to school?"

"I'll put the dishes and trivia in storage. Get all my personal stuff out of Sherry's way. Dave and Sherry can use the furniture until I decide where my life will take me. They don't have dining room furniture, anyway."

"So where will home be for you in the meantime?"

"Toronto. We have a condo there. Dad bought it when Dave started at U of T. Sherry's brother shared it with us and has been living with Dave this last year. I'll move there after the wedding...while they're on honeymoon. Actually, I hope to leave in early August so I can have a short holiday before I hit the books."

"So, you're leaving me?"

"I'll have somebody trained before then. We still have three months, you know."

He opened his mouth as if to speak, then changed his mind. She was right, they still had three months. Anything could happen in three months. Meantime, there was a party on Friday night, and he…and she…would be there. "Will you let me escort you to the party?" he asked before he could stop himself.

"I'm sorry. The judge has ordered a limo. Bob's folks have changed their plans; Bob wanted to celebrate together with Dave, so it will be larger than planned. Why not come to the house and join us?"

"That would be presumptuous of me."

"Not at all. We'd all love to have you…lots of room in the limo."

"Maybe I'll just see you there. Save the waltzes for me."

<hr />

The party was indeed larger than he expected. The huge ballroom buzzed with activity. Dave spotted him at once and came to escort him to their table. He was relieved to be seated between Lee and Dave. Sherry on the other side of Dave…then her brother…her parents. The judge and his wife were seated next to Lee and kept up a running conversation. It promised to be a lively party. He was glad he had come after all…glad that he knew how to dress for this sort of thing…how to dance. He wondered who had looked after the seating arrangements; obviously not Sherry's brother, Bob. He could hardly keep his eyes off Lee.

No small wonder, he thought. *That green silk gown that just matches her eyes; her hair all piled up that way, with diamonds peeking out here and there.*

"They haven't spared any expense," he commented to Dave, as the platters of turkey, beef, ham and ribs began to arrive. "Who will be able to dance after this?"

The short program was lively and entertaining. The graduates telling war stories on each other…the jokes…the accolades…Bob's parents giving a history of their son's life. The judge enjoyed his role as MC…a little too much, Lee thought. She was both surprised and pleased as her brother rose and gave thanks to all those who had enabled him to graduate. He told of his parents' encouragement, and Judge Ben and Aunt Maude. He paused then as his voice caught. "And," he began, now almost in tears, "I want to say thanks to my little sis." He looked down at Lee. "Without her sacrifice…quitting school to care for Dad this past year…I would not have graduated." Then turning to his sister, he continued, "Lee, I am committed to see you through…the party next year will be for you."

She looked down quickly as tears blurred her vision, and a burst of applause filled the room. Brett gently squeezed her hand under the table, and the judge gave her a hug.

The orchestra, finally in tune, cut in with a lively two-step, and Dave and Sherry were quick to lead. "They've done that a time or two." Brett turned to Lee, only to see Bob guiding her swiftly toward the floor. *They've done that a time or two, too,* he thought as he watched them in perfect step. A polka followed…then a jive. Still they had not returned to the table. He was more than relieved when Lee finally excused herself and returned to her seat next to him.

"Enough already," she said, laughing. "Think I'm too old for that fast stuff."

They chatted amiably as they sat out the next few numbers. "Time to waltz," the judge announced and helped Aunt Maude to her feet.

Brett looked questioningly at Lee. "Is it time to waltz?" he asked.

She smiled consent, and he rose and held her chair.

She was surprised at how comfortable she was with Brett…how easily they moved together. He smelled fresh and clean…like soap and aftershave. She had never been this close to him before and found herself enjoying his nearness.

"You take my breath away," he murmured, pulling her closer as the lights dimmed. She resisted the pressure to rest her head on his shoulder, then eased away as the waltz ended and another began. "Can we do this all night?" he asked, looking down into her eyes.

Her eyes were warm and soft as they looked up into his.

"Now, now, no time to be selfish," the judge cut in, as he and Maude exchanged partners with the younger couple.

"I can hardly believe it's almost midnight," she commented as she found herself finally back in his arms. "No wonder I'm about done in."

"Lee." He lowered his lips to her ear. "Will you let me take you home?"

Again her eyes looked up into his. They were still soft and warm…but now there was a question.

"Oh, Brett," she said softly.

"Is that 'Oh Brett, yes'?"

She looked up at him through her lashes, then slowly nodded.

He pulled slowly onto her driveway and turned off the ignition. "Drawbridge gone up?"

She turned toward him from her side of the car. "You've got to stop using that drawbridge…."

"No. You do, Lee. Tell me what happened between the party and here. I thought for a while there when we were dancing, that the drawbridge was open…and maybe I was on it. Now I feel like I've been pushed off into the moat. Explain," he added as she hesitated.

"I'm fond of you, Brett; you know I am." She could see his eyes in the moonlight…wide and questioning. "I admire and respect you so much. Obviously you are respected by the entire legal community…your clients are increasing by leaps and bounds."

"What does that have to do with us?"

"That's the *lawyer* I know. The *man* inside…I don't know…we only met a few weeks ago."

"So how will you get to know me if you find it so hard to spend time with me?"

"We spend at least eight hours together, five days a week."

"That's not the same thing…and you know it." He slipped an arm around her shoulders.

"You are something else," she said, allowing him to pull her close.

"I thought I was being pretty up front." He planted a kiss in her hair as she turned her mouth away.

Dave and Sherry arrived in the limo and went into the house as though they didn't see his car in the driveway.

He caught her hand and kissed it, then lifting her chin, he looked into her eyes, long and deeply. She turned to avoid his kiss and he caressed her temple...her cheek.

"Kitten," he whispered, "a soft little kitten."

CHAPTER ELEVEN

"Morning kitten." He blew a kiss as he breezed into the office.

"Brett!" she exclaimed in mock horror. "Behave yourself."

He grinned. "I haven't looked forward to Monday morning this much in my entire life. Dave in yet?"

"Oh, sure. He's been rattling around in there for at least an hour...trying to remember his name."

"Great! Will you pour us a coffee and tell him I'd like to see him in my office? I'll need his input; he's all studied up on young offenders. We've got to keep this thing in juvenile court...those kids don't deserve life behind bars."

No wonder he's such a good lawyer...knows how to maximize his resources...how to keep staff onside. Dave will be happy here, she concluded.

They were both smiling as they emerged an hour later and headed to the courthouse.

"See you around noon; get us a sandwich." Brett winked as he swung through the door.

Just a couple of big boys! she mused...then added a prayer, *Give them wisdom, Lord.*

They returned triumphant as the sandwiches arrived.

"That's round one." Dave grinned.

"Lee, I'd like you to join us over lunch. There are some things...." He paused and Lee noted his stress as he continued. "There are some things about this trial that are most unusual. I've known the defendant, Tony Cortez...since I was a boy. I am probably the only one who can identify the knife—a switchblade with a jewelled handle. I saw it at the police station. I remember when he bought it…how he got the money…saw him use it dozens of times. He must really have been rattled to leave it behind; maybe he hasn't committed murder before. As you know, Lee, his mother would like me to defend him. Not only do I know in my heart that he is guilty…I believe he needs to be put away…stopped from preying on young boys." He stopped as Lee gasped.

"So you're the only link between the knife and the accused?" Dave interjected. "Do I sense a bargaining chip?"

"Very well put. If I bring this evidence to the court…and I must…I will destroy any possible defense he could have. He'll get life!"

"And the boys?" she asked.

"We're going to bargain for a suspended sentence. Course we won't get it, but we may get a reduced sentence. The best we can hope for is two years in a detention center…it beats four for Rob Chambers…he's seventeen, and five for Coombs and Dewalt."

"Lee, can you call the parents of our three; have them meet us here Tuesday afternoon."

She shuddered as she looked again at the picture of Tony Cortez…a killer? Perhaps. But also a human being…someone who had been born on the wrong side of the tracks and learned early how to fend for himself…how to take advantage. What chance did he have with a mother like his? Did he have a father? Probably not. Her heart went out to him. *No wonder I don't want to be a lawyer*, she mused. *I'd let him get away with murder.*

She watched Dave and Brett excitedly planning their strategy for defense. Did they care that a man would go to prison for life with no help and no hope? Was Brett enjoying…? She couldn't go there. She would like to ask him about his association with Tony and his mother; he had been awfully closed about that part of his life, but she dared not…not until he was ready to deal with his past.

"Wish I could avoid that convention this week," Brett commented as she laid a file on his desk. "Couldn't come at a worse time. Guess I'd best put in an appearance a time or two. Did you reserve a couple sets of tickets for dinner on Wednesday?" he asked, his mind already on the file in front of him.

Janet Dewalt arrived early, with her usual flourish, demanding to see Brett before the meeting. She had a private matter to discuss.

"I am sorry, Mrs. Dewalt. Mr. Walker will not be taking calls between now and four o'clock. He's in a meeting. Could I offer you a fresh coffee while you wait, or would you prefer to come back a little later?"

"Really, now! If you'd just let me talk to him for a moment…."

"I am sorry," Lee reiterated to the agitated woman.

"Well, I never!" she muttered as the door closed behind her.

"I'd like you to join us for the meeting, Lee, and maybe we could borrow a couple of chairs from the library."

She admired the way he did things; actually, was there anything about this man that she didn't admire? Except…maybe…? No time to think about that now. She hastened to make sure there would be coffee for everybody as the parents began to arrive.

She was surprised when *Dave* began the briefing…going over the charges…the ground covered thus far…the morning's victory— keeping the case in the juvenile court. They were working on having the charges reduced to breaking and entering. "They may get a few years in a detention center, but it would be a far cry from second-degree murder with a life sentence," he pointed out. He had obviously done his homework. *He's already one fantastic lawyer*, she mused. The smile on Brett's face seconded the motion.

Brett took over and explained the circumstances of the arrest of Tony Cortez and its implications for the boys. Lee noted that he did not include the *bargaining chip* he intended to use in their defense.

His request for a bail hearing was pending. Meantime, the boys would remain in custody.

The five parents remained silent. Obviously they did not comprehend the seriousness of the crime, or the amount of work that had already been done on their behalf. Clearly, they felt their offspring were innocent…a small thing…using a bank card to get refunds in a sporting-goods store. The implications of the murder were beyond them. Lee found herself disappointed in their reaction. They expected their kids would be released…they were missing school. She wondered if they were thinking *perhaps with a different lawyer…?*

Only Janet Dewalt smiled and praised their efforts on behalf of the boys. *She's still after him,* Lee thought, as the others filed out and she asked for a private counsel with Brett. She was amazed at how graciously he declined.

"I have an engagement with Brett Walker," the heavy French accent purred.

"Who shall I tell him is here, Madame?"

"Mademoiselle….Madamoiselle Jeanette Bouvier. He will know. He is expecting me."

I don't think so, Lee thought as she relayed the news to Brett.

"Madame LaBlanc, how nice to see you again," he spoke guardedly as he came through the door.

"Madamoiselle Bouvier," she corrected him, as she rushed to throw her arms around him and plant a kiss on the cheek he turned. "Mon amoureux homme! I have come to take you to supper; of course you got my message?" Her perfume filled the room as she tossed her stole over her shoulder and cast a suspicious glance at Lee.

"Message?" he asked.

"Ah, but of course, on your voice mail; I told you I would be here by five." She continued to hold onto Brett, bombarding him with endearments in French.

"When did you leave it, Madamoiselle?"

"Some time ago."

"I heard the phone ring but we were in the meeting," Lee explained, trying desperately to close down her computer and leave the office.

"I'm really sorry for the confusion," she heard him apologize as she exited.

"But I'm afraid you are mistaken," he struggled to extricate himself. "I am not able to join you this evening; I have other plans," he finished as he removed her arms from around his neck. *Why does this always happen to me?* he wondered vaguely as Dave hurried through pretending not to notice.

Chapter Twelve

"Isn't it time you were heading home?" he asked, looking at his watch.

"Not really. Is there a reason why you'd like to get rid of me by 4:30?"

"Of course not. Just thought you'd like a little more time to get ready."

"Ready?"

"Yeah. Don't ladies usually need an extra hour or two?"

"I'm going somewhere?"

"Lee! Cut it out! I thought we were going to the convention reception and banquet."

She was stunned. "Are you talking about *you and me?*"

"Yeah, and Dave and Sherry. Come on now, you ordered the tickets a week ago."

"I didn't know who they were for. It never entered my head that you planned for me to go. I had even forgotten it was tonight until Mademoiselle called and said she'd pick you up at 6:30. Have you checked your screen? I left the message from Janet that she's expecting you for supper at 7:00. How many women do you think you can handle in one evening?"

"You know I'm not going to do either of those things, Lee. Will you call…? Never mind, guess that's no job for you. I am sorry…guess the week just sort of took me over. Will you forgive me for forgetting to ask you. Just thought you knew. Didn't Dave say anything?"

"Haven't talked to him all week."

"Will you come, Lee? If you left right now…could you be ready by 6:30…or 7:00? They have sort of a reception for an hour before supper; it won't matter if we're late."

"What do ladies wear to this sort of thing? Is it formal?"

"Yeah, sort of. Would you wear that lovely green gown you wore to Dave's party? And all those little diamonds in your hair?"

She stood for a few moments with her hands covering her face. *Drawbridge is definitely up*, he decided.

"Fine," she managed at last, "we'll see what we can do."

Call Sherry, find out what she's wearing, she told herself as she pulled into the driveway; *and call Marita and see if she can do my hair. Maybe I should call Aunt Maude…she's gone to these things for years.*

❦

"Why my dear, you'll be a knockout whatever you wear. That lovely green the other night…and perhaps a fur…most ladies wear a stole or a shawl or some such."

"I don't really have an abundance of fur, Aunt Maude."

"Don't you still have your mother's things, dear?"

Suddenly Lee knew what she would wear. Yes, she'd wear the green, and that new fur stole that Dad had bought Mom for Christmas. She had not lived to wear it. Lee had always wanted to ask Dad if she should take it back to the store but didn't have the heart to bring up the subject. Quickly she flew to the closet…still as her mother had left it. Tears stung her eyes as she gently removed the gorgeous silver-tipped fur. How her mom had loved it! How lovely she would have looked in it! Dad would have been so proud! *Well, perhaps tonight they'll both be proud!*

He whistled softly as she opened the door. "Lee…thank you for forgiving my blunder. Maybe you don't need to hear it from me…but I need to say it…you're a very beautiful woman! The belle of the ball!"

"That must be because I'm being escorted by the most eligible lawyer in London. However will I deal with all the competition when I have no phone to put on hold?"

"And no place to run?" he smirked. *Drawbridge is coming down*, he mused.

Dave and Sherry met them in the portico. Sherry was her beautiful self—blond hair piled high with small ringlets peeking out here and there. She had also worn her green silk—darker than Lee's. "You always look stunning," Lee commented.

"You, too." Her friend smiled back.

The Convention Center swarmed with couples dressed in finery and jewels. Lee couldn't help but notice how proudly Brett escorted her through the milieu, stopping here and there to chat and introduce her. He was surprised how well known she was in legal circles, and Dave seemed to be chatting with many of his father's former clients and friends.

"Now just look who's here. Our very own little Miss Lee." She recognized another of her father's old friends, Mr. Foster, of Foster, Jamieson and Co. "Now they tell me," he began, "that this young man has lured you out of that house and into his office?" He looked at Brett.

"I am happy to tell you that you have good hearing, Mr. Foster," the younger lawyer admitted.

"Good. Well now, Miss Lee, I've been talking to your brother...I understand this Mr. Walker has gotten his hooks into him, too."

"Right again!"

"Now that's all fine and well, but I also hear that you plan to return to U of T and complete your LLB, and I just want you to know that I would love to have you article with my firm next year. I know you'll get all those offers from Bay Street, and all that group, but they don't hold a candle to what we have to offer right here in London. Now, do I have a promise that you'll let that simmer on the back burner?"

"Yes, Mr. Foster...consider it done."

"You're a very fortunate young man, Brett Walker. Not just one Stevenson...but two." He walked away shaking his head.

Brett smiled down at her. "I already know that."

"So there she is. I hoped I would see you here." She felt Brett's fingers tighten on her elbow as the man continued. "I see you have registered for my *Advocacy* course...we have a perfectly wonderful time in that class...well, hello, Brett."

Brett nodded. "Hello, Lonnie. You're still in the teaching business, I see."

"Of course, of course, with such sweet young things coming every year…is there any other vocation?"

She felt the pressure on her arm to move along, and the professor smirked, as he added, "No need to worry…we'll have *plenty* of time to get acquainted."

"Are you really registered for his class?"

"Is there some reason I shouldn't be?"

Supper was announced and he declined to comment as they moved toward the dining room.

"Heh, Brett Walker, I just met your articling student. Why don't you bring him along to breakfast on Wednesday?" Leanne recognized a young lawyer with the Foster firm.

"He'll be along once he's settled."

So Brett is going to the prayer breakfast…with the judge, Mr. Foster, and a couple of others. Funny, he hasn't said a thing.

He didn't say anything now, either, as he escorted her toward the table to join Dave and Sherry.

"Ah, mon cher homme, est-ce vous?"

"Good evening, Madame LaBlanc. Have you met Miss Stevenson?" Lee noticed he was careful to keep her between himself and the Madame.

"Oui, Oui," she managed, as her eyes flashed angrily. In a moment she brushed past and was lost in the crowd.

Lee looked up and caught a twinkle in his eyes, as he smiled down at her.

Drawbridge is definitely down, he decided.

"Can I interest you in a drive…and maybe a stroll in Springbank Park?" he asked as they left the parkade. "The night is young and a full moon on the Thames really shouldn't be wasted."

She smiled consent, wondering how her silver-strapped sandals would do in the park.

He parked in view of the river and they sat silently watching the ripples sparkle and dance in the moonlight.

"Did you enjoy the evening?" he asked at last.

"Yes. Very much. Met a lot of folk I haven't seen in a while...made some new acquaintances. Good to see Mr. Foster. Haven't seen him in a long time."

"He apparently thinks I've hit the jackpot with two Stevensons on board. A very discerning gentleman, I would say."

She smiled. "Or perhaps an exaggerating one!"

He reached for her hand. "Lee, I want to thank you for coming with me tonight...especially in the circumstances. I have never enjoyed this event...feel like I have to be there...it's the event of the year for legal everything. I thoroughly enjoyed tonight...having you there was very special for me."

"I'm glad, Brett. Can I ask you why you were disturbed about my registering for Lonnie Hencken's class in *Advocacy*?"

He sat for a time as though arguing with himself, then, "I don't think I can answer that right now."

"Is he not a good instructor?"

"I'm not sure. Don't think I'm qualified to answer that."

"But you have reservations?"

"I would have to say I do. Maybe we should talk to Dave and get his input."

She nodded as he continued, "What did you think of Mr. Foster's offer?"

"Definitely something that should be considered if I decide to go into law for real. What did you think?"

"He obviously knows you quite well...wanted to get his bid in early. You won't forget that Dave and I...? Even if you decide to article somewhere else, Lee...."

What he leaves out speaks volumes, she thought. "I won't forget, Brett. But at this point I think we might all benefit from my articling somewhere else. Whether that should be in London will have to be decided if that time comes."

He nodded as he slipped his arm around her shoulders. "Kitten...you are such a soft little kitten...and that lovely fur! Was that a gift?"

"I guess you could say that."

He raised an eyebrow. "A special man in your life?"

"Not anymore."

"I'm glad to hear that."

"Don't be. It was a Christmas gift from my dad to my mom. She died on Boxing Day. I always wanted to ask him if he'd like me to return it to the store, but he was so broken up about Mom…didn't want any of her things removed. I didn't have the heart to broach the subject. Now Dave and I have to…." Her voice broke.

He pulled her close, resting her head on his shoulder. *She did this for me*, he thought. *I've been busy showing her off…and she's been bleeding all over the carpet.* "I feel awfully selfish…enjoying myself so much this evening…when you're hurting. Forgive me."

"Not your fault. My own choice entirely."

"You're very special to me, kitten. I'm not looking forward to your leaving."

"You seem to have a lot of special ladies in your life, Brett. I would think one less…."

"Hold it! I don't have any other ladies in my life. I haven't even dated…."

"Honestly, Brett. How many calls have you gotten in the last two weeks?"

"I have never dated any of those women. Jeannette Bouvier has chased me for years, since second-year university. She shows up in the strangest places…looking for a man. Whatever brought her to the law convention is anybody's guess. She's apparently divorced…again. Poor LaBlanc…she had him so bewitched…he didn't know what hit him. Course it couldn't last!"

She looked up at him slightly amused. "You don't have to explain to me, Brett; your social life really is your own business."

"I wish you cared, Lee. I wish you cared if somebody else was after me."

"I care about you, Brett. I care a great deal. I just don't think I'm ready…I'm kind of numb from all that's happened in my life in the last eighteen months. I think I'll need some time…."

"You want to keep your options open for university…?"

"You didn't hear a word I said, Brett Walker. I'm not ready for a relationship. My emotions are in an upheaval. Guess I didn't really have time to grieve for Mom; I was too busy caring for Dad. Now I find myself in grief…big time! I seem to cry at the drop of a hat. Then Brodie…now I need to move. Didn't really think it would be a big deal…but it's the only home I've ever known…and I want to get out of the way…." She was teary again.

"O God," he prayed as he pulled her close, "please help…I don't know how to comfort her." It took a moment before he realized he had spoken out loud. "I'm sorry, kitten. I don't mean to push. Forgive me."

She nodded against his shoulder. "You're a special man," she whispered.

CHAPTER THIRTEEN

"Mornin' Kitten, Dave in yet?"

"Sure enough." She nodded without looking up.

"Will you see if he's free. Gotta get those kids out of that jail. They've missed enough school for one year." He disappeared into his office.

She poured their coffee as they discussed the reduced charge— Breaking and Entering.

"Do you have time to slip down and arrange for bail, Dave? My morning is pretty full."

Dave nodded. "Brief me on the procedure…." she heard him ask as she returned to the outer office.

Thank you, God, she whispered. *Thank you that they get along better than brothers.*

I'm really going to miss all this, she told herself between phone calls. *Maybe I should just learn to be a legal secretary and leave it at that.*

"I'm glad that day's over," she admitted as they sat over a late cup of coffee. The agency sent over four gals…I gave them each this little questionnaire. None of them were terribly qualified, but this one has possibilities." She handed the file to Brett as she spoke. "Would you like me to set up an interview?"

"Is this the blonde?" he asked with as much eagerness as he could muster.

"Sorry." She laughed. "You would be, too."

"Shucks. I'm disappointed. You left her out on purpose," he kidded.

"You got that right. Want to see her answers. She left most of them out. Said she does much better when she's interviewed by men. I almost lost her when Dave came through. She wanted to know if he was married. I said 'almost,' and she thought she could go with that."

"So...maybe I *should* interview her. Got her file?"

"Would you like me to set that up? Or would you like to call her yourself?" she asked, surrendering the file.

He reddened slightly. "I was kidding, Lee. You're supposed to get upset...yell...jump around...throw stuff...."

Without hesitation she jumped up and sent the files skidding across the desk, spilling the contents on the floor, as she yelled, "You're not having that blonde for a secretary...DO YOU HEAR ME? You have three others to choose from...DO YOU HEAR ME?"

She followed Brett's gaze to where Dave stood in the doorway...speechless.

"Can we help you with something?" Brett asked nonchalantly.

"I'm not sure," he said, backing away in confusion. "Guess I forgot what I came for."

"Will that do?" she asked.

Brett grinned. "Well, it's a start." He was still grinning as he picked up the scattered papers and tried to replace materials in the proper files. "Worth it," he assured himself. "Good thing she'd finished her coffee."

She smiled as she returned to her desk. *Would love to be a mouse in the corner when Dave tries to describe this scene to Sherry.*

"Mornin' kitten," he greeted as he came through the door.

"Good morning, Mr. Walker."

It took him a moment to realize that the formal greeting was occasioned by the presence of a client. He continued to his office, much to the amusement of Mrs. VanClive.

Lee poured his morning coffee and escorted the beautifully coiffed matron into his office. She smiled graciously as she held out her cup for a refill.

She was still smiling a half hour later when she emerged, and bid Lee a good morning.

"I've found you a secretary," she began, as the door closed behind Mrs. VanClive.

"So…is it the blonde?"

"Well…sort of."

"Sort of…you got this one?…or you got one sort-of blonde?"

"Got one sort-of blonde."

"Do I get to interview her, or are you just going to foist her on me blind?"

"You really don't need to interview her. She'll do nicely."

"Do we have a file…a picture…a name?"

"All of the above, but you really won't need the file. How about Mrs. Beck?"

"Becky? You're kidding! Thought her husband was dying."

"So did the doctors, but the tests have now come back negative. Guess he had a bad gall-bladder attack. Had to have it out. She wants to come back to work…needs the job. I thought you'd be delighted."

"Delighted as I *can* be at losing you."

"When would you like her to come in? I thought if she came a week or so before I left that we could go over some of the new systems I've put in place…will make it a lot easier for her, and for you, too."

"Go for it. I appreciate your care in all this. I really do…even if she is only 'sorta blonde.'" He grinned.

"I'd be careful if I were you…unless of course you *like* picking your files up off the floor." She turned to go, then asked, "Would it be okay to have a small reception to welcome her back?"

"What do you have in mind?"

"Maybe just some special cakes, goodies, coffee for the clients who come. We could invite the lawyers down the hall…nothing big."

"I like that idea. I like it very much…but Lee, I want you to let us say 'goodbye' to you. Can we at least go for supper…the four of us…as a special 'thank you' from the office?"

She was surprised. He hadn't asked for a date in the last few weeks and with all the talk of blondes, she assumed he had turned his attention elsewhere.

"Maybe you'd like to ask Dave," she said, stalling. "He's the one under pressure with the wedding coming up. I have time…and the thought is really special."

"Shouldn't you be leaving for court this morning…on that Lewthwaite Estate?"

"Don't think so…unless you forgot to put it in my day minder."

"I put it in. Should have reminded you ten minutes ago."

He flipped open the small electronic gadget. No response. "Oh boy! Battery is gone…guess I've lost a year of entries. Serves me right for postponing the inevitable."

"Shall I pick one up for you over the lunch hour?"

"I'll have to give that some thought. Can't imagine myself starting all over—entering all that data. Maybe let it go for now," he suggested as he hurriedly left for the courthouse.

⚬❦⚬

The phone rang as she picked up their coffee cups. "Why, yes," she answered graciously, "he's right here."

In answer to his questioning look, she responded, "Mrs. Rosita Cortez."

He gave her a long look, then picked up the receiver. "This is Brett Walker," she heard as she made a hasty retreat. The conversation was short and she heard the phone click.

"Lee, I want you to come into my office." She hurried to comply. "What do you mean by setting me up like this? You knew I didn't want to talk to her."

She looked up at him like a naughty child. "You needed to talk to her, Brett. She called all day yesterday…wants you to defend Tony."

"You know I'm the chief witness for the prosecution. That's why three boys are going to walk today. They're innocent, Lee. Tony is guilty…of murder. So what do you want me to do?" he challenged as she sat silently. "Do you think he should get off?"

"Of course not. A man is dead. But I'm concerned, Brett…."

"You're concerned about the world, Lee. Ever thought of going into social work?"

His barb hit the mark. "No, but I am considering becoming counsel for the defense. Besides, you didn't let me finish. You seem to be enjoying your role far too much here. You're so vindictive. This man…this Tony needs help…somebody to care…somebody to show him the way. Guess what he really needs is a faith to give his life order and direction…."

"The court and the press would love it."

"Yes, they would, and Brett Walker would accuse him of trying to pre-empt justice by 'getting religion.'"

He flinched.

"I'm sorry; that was a low blow," she confessed. "Forgive me, please."

"If you forgive mine about the social worker."

She nodded. "Brett, what if you visited Tony in the jail…suggested to him that he needs to plead guilty. He's going to be convicted anyway. Couldn't you…I don't know…couldn't you speak to the sentencing…isn't there something…?"

He sat for a time with his eyes closed. Then looking across the desk at her, he conceded, "This Christian life is a pretty complicated business."

"Who said it was easy?"

"Sure looks like it when I watch you."

"I wish."

"I'll go and see Tony. That's all I'm promising for now."

CHAPTER FOURTEEN

"It's one beautiful evening," she commented as he helped her into the car.

"Beautiful evening…beautiful woman! Is that another new dress?"

She gasped as they pulled up to Michael's on the Thames. "Brett…this is really special. How did you know I always wanted to come here?"

"Got a little help from Dave. I think he and Sherry could have come, you know. My guess is…they thought I really wanted you all to myself." He paused. "I did want you all to myself."

He waited until they were seated and then continued, "Lee, I am so sorry for our exchange yesterday concerning Tony and his mom."

"I'm sorry, too, Brett. We haven't had one of those in a long time. I'm sorry for getting in your way; it was none of my business…."

"I visited Tony last night."

She looked up in surprise. "You did!"

"Didn't you want me to?" She nodded as he went on. "It was good for both of us. You are right; he does need help…a whole lot more than a lawyer can provide. He doesn't seem to have any ground beneath his feet…nothing to keep him out of the quicksand…no rules of the road…no morals…no faith in anything but his wit and his knife."

She nodded. "Will you help him?"

"Don't know yet. Only if he pleads guilty. He's thinking it over…will discuss it with his mamma. He knows they have his knife…doesn't know I'm the only one who can identify it. He's more broken up about the murder than I would have given him credit for. He's pretty sure he'll get life in prison. I realize now that I need to keep in touch with him, Lee. I'm glad you pushed me on this. I have some history to deal with…I'll tell you about it one day…but not tonight. That's far too much shop talk already for such a special night."

"Thank you for sharing with me," she said softly.

Drawbridge is definitely down, he mused with satisfaction. "That reception was one special idea. I have never seen Becky that excited in the five years she worked for me. I would never have thought of that."

"It was fun, wasn't it? Can't believe how many showed up. Thought I'd have to order more goodies before the day was done."

"So you're all packed and moved; didn't even give me a chance to help."

"Sorry. I didn't want to impose on you when Dave had to get the rest of his stuff from Toronto; it worked well for him to take the van and deliver my stuff at the same time."

"The offer is still good. If there's anything I can do for you, Lee…anything I can bring down for you…I'd love an excuse to come and visit you."

"You don't need an excuse, Brett. I'd love to see you any time."

His eyes met hers across the table. *Is she putting me on?* But her eyes were warm and inviting. Too bad he'd waited so long. Now only four days till the wedding…and she'd be gone. "Will you keep in touch with me?" he asked.

"Would you like that?"

"You know I would."

"I didn't know, Brett. In fact I thought perhaps you'd found…that maybe you were interested in…well you do seem to prefer blondes," she finished lamely.

"Oh, kitten." He shook his head. "I just try to get a rise out of you once in a while. It never works…."

"I thought it worked pretty well! Would just love to know what Dave told Sherry. He asked me how we were getting along. Wanted to know if everything was okay. I assured him it was."

They both laughed, remembering the temper tantrum.

"This seafood is delicious. What did you order?"

"Can't remember. Sounded good at the time. Everything is good here, I'm told. So…I gather you're registered for all your classes?"

"Pretty well. I did talk to Dave about Lonnie's *Advocacy* class. Apparently there is room for a good deal of caution."

"That's what I've heard. Will you let me know if there are any irregularities?"

"I'm not sure what I'm looking for. How will I know an irregularity from a regularity in a strange class…a strange prof…?"

"Some profs are stranger than others. You'll know if it's irregular. Will you keep us posted if you're feeling uncomfortable…?"

"I'm always uncomfortable when I'm stretched beyond my comfort zone. You may get a call every second week." She laughed. "Anyway, I'll do my best. Good enough?"

"I'd love it," he assured her. "Where did the time go? It's almost nine. I did promise Dave and Sherry we'd be there for coffee." He slipped her wrap around her shoulders and let his arm linger around her waist as they left the restaurant.

"Sorry, I need to stop at Judge Davis's for a minute or two. Will you come in with me?"

"No, Brett. For goodness sake…look at the cars…they have company. Why don't you just go to the back door and get what you want?"

"They'd ask why I didn't bring you. Come…please." He held out his hand.

"No, Brett. That's not proper…crashing in on somebody's party. I'll wait in the car."

"Please…kitten."

"No."

"Sure gonna be a lot of disappointed folk in there. The party is for you."

"Brett Walker…you are putting me on!" she accused as the front door opened and Dave waved them to come in. "Well, I'll be…" she added as she hurried to comply.

The house was filled with family and friends…good food… delicacies…music…laughter…dancing…well-wishes and advice. She stood in shock beside a smiling Brett.

"Really, Dave, how does one come up with all this a few days before his wedding?"

"You know the judge and Aunt Maude! They were already planning…and when they found out that we were…it all fell into place."

"This has been an evening to remember." She took his arm as he walked her to the door. "Thank you for your part in it…the special time together in the restaurant…the exotic food…."

Drawbridge is definitely down. "Kitten…my beautiful kitten," he whispered, holding her close. She was warm and responsive as he nuzzled her neck, her ear, trailing little kisses over her temple and down her cheek. She looked up at him and in the dim light from the porch he could see the beautiful grey-green of her eyes, wide and questioning. "May I kiss you goodnight?" he whispered, his heart pounding.

She hesitated, then lifted her mouth. He knew he would never forget the thrill of holding her in his arms, her lips warm and responsive. He kissed her gently, holding her as though he couldn't bear to have it end.

CHAPTER FIFTEEN

Why haven't I come sooner? In fact, why haven't I been coming here every week?
Brett questioned himself as the usher settled him in the aisle seat, half
way down the sanctuary. The strains of organ music lent a note of
reverence...something from Bach, he guessed. He glanced about
him—huge   white   bells...pink   and   white
streamers...roses...lilies...candles. He had never seen anything quite
like it.

So...today Dave and Sherry would become Mr. and Mrs....after
loving each other all those years. He guessed maybe he had a few things
to learn about love.

He smiled, thinking of the past few months with Dave. They had
been an adventure...an adventure in living. No wonder Sherry loved
him...wanted him. *I want him, too,* he admitted to himself. *I'll talk to him
about a partnership once he gets this honeymoon over with. Can't have Foster, or
anybody else, getting the jump on him. Whatever would I do without him? What did
I do before he came?*

Lee is right, he concluded, *she and Dave really are a lot alike. Need to get
some things nailed down with her too...* the warmth of her kiss lingered on his
lips...the smell of her perfume...*that wretched Foster!*

His reverie was broken as the pastor entered from the front of the
sanctuary, followed by Dave and his four groomsmen. He recognized
Bob Wilson as the best man, the other three were strangers. Dave was
more than handsome in his black tux—he was distinguished, flanked
by his groomsmen in grey.

The music changed slightly as the bridesmaids appeared in slow and graceful procession. Three identically gowned young women—all in soft, filmy pink with long trailing bouquets of pink and white roses with fern and…something else he couldn't identify. He didn't recognize any of them. Then, suddenly, there she was—the maid of honour…her gown…her roses a slightly more intense shade of pink. Lee…his Lee…if only…maybe by this time next year…! She moved gracefully down the aisle without seeming to know he was there.

Suddenly the organ burst forth in joyful mirth; the doors opened as hundreds of guests stood to their feet as one. *Here comes the bride!*

He was happy for the aisle seat as the little ring bearer and petite, blonde flower girl made their way toward the front. She scattered tiny rose petals as she walked. He noted that some fell on the white carpet, others caught on her pink frilly gown.

And then there was Sherry. She was beautiful at the worst of times…but nothing had prepared him to see her in her bridal gown. Rows of tiny pearls in her hair, on her gown…in her bouquet of deep pink and white roses. She was radiant. Her father escorted her proudly!

And Dave…his face aglow…standing tall…waiting.

Brett found himself praying…praying that all would be as wonderful for Dave and Sherry as they had planned.

They paused midway down the aisle. "Who gives this woman to this man?" He heard the voice of Pastor Somerville.

"Her mother and I," her father responded.

When I get married I want a wedding just like this one, Brett mused, then felt his heart pounding as Dave shook hands with his father-to-be and, offering his arm to his bride, escorted her to the platform.

The remainder of the ceremony flew by in a blur. The day flew by in a blur…the long reception line…everyone kissing the bride and her maids…introductions…hundreds of friends and relatives at the punch and hors d'oeuvres reception…the lovely turkey and ham banquet for close relatives and friends. The toasts and advice to bride and groom had been priceless. He had been one of the special guests—invited to enjoy it all. *I guess this is what family is all about*, he concluded.

And always there was Lee…attending Sherry…looking her lovely self. But she would be gone…if not tomorrow, then probably Monday.

She said he could come and see her. He would have to get some things settled before then. He just couldn't go on wondering. One thing was certain…he would meet her in church tomorrow…and afterward maybe…just maybe….

Monday would be a down day with both Dave and Lee gone. So…it was back to him and Mrs. Beck…Becky. How fast the months had flown…four months…gone in a breath. Like they'd never been. Good that Lee got Becky up to speed on everything. They would do okay…until Dave got back in a couple of weeks. Amazing how much he'd come to depend on him.

"Before you go, everyone," the voice of Sherry's father cut through his thoughts, "we want to invite you to stop by for dinner tomorrow…help us with all this delectable food. Our bride and groom will be gone…but we can still celebrate. Shall we say about one o'clock?"

"I'm going to help Sherry change," she whispered as she brushed past him on her way out. "See you tomorrow."

He sat for a few moments before turning the key in the ignition. He felt alone again…the echoes of *the dream*. Funny, it always seemed to be this way for him…and yet….

CHAPTER SIXTEEN

"I'm feeling a tad bit guilty for not staying and helping Sherry's folks with the tidying up," she admitted as he opened the car door for her.

"Aunt Maude has it all well in hand…a whole fleet of volunteers in the kitchen. Besides, they sort of shoo-ed you off; figured you'd done your share. Okay if we just drive for a while…stop here and there…spend the day together?"

"Love to. Whatever you'd like is okay with me. I am pretty weary, but happy…everything just went off like clockwork. A lot of things can go wrong with so much to organize."

"Where do you think they went, Lee?"

"Well, they expected to spend last night at the condo in Toronto; that's why I'm not going there until tomorrow. Today they may have caught a flight somewhere…maybe Hawaii where it isn't too hot. That's my first guess. Second, is that they'll drive to Quebec and rent a houseboat for a couple of weeks; third is that they may just drive to the Maritimes and enjoy sightseeing and beaching. They've been really secretive."

"So what makes you suspect one of those three?"

"Brochures that I've seen in Dave's office. Sherry's new bathing suit. Dave having the car all checked over in the last week makes me wonder if it's going farther than Toronto. They'll enjoy whatever they do. They're really tuned in to each other's likes and dislikes."

"I've noticed that. How many years does it take to develop a relationship like that?"

"Took them about twenty plus." She laughed. We weren't in kindergarten yet when Sherry would come to play with me and spend all afternoon playing Barbie dolls with Dave. She would dress Barbie…he would dress Ken…then they would go camping. Then she would play marbles with him. She got so good at it she took all of her brother's marbles away. I hated when Dave was at home and she came to play…she preferred him to me. I was always the odd one in the triangle."

"What about Bob? Where did he fit in?"

"He never did. He was on a different wavelength than any of us. Didn't really like our games or toys. We just never hit it off…at least not until we were old enough for sports. Dave and Sherry left him out too. Dave would go to her music recitals; she would go to his basketball games. They learned to include others at school, but they still always preferred each other over everybody else."

"Interesting!"

"He was a pretty young teenager when he started having Sunday dinners at Sherry's house. Her folks just knew if he didn't come there, Sherry would be at our house. I'm really surprised they waited this long to get married. Some maturity there."

"You got that right. Guess they never worried about losing each other?"

"Didn't seem to cross their minds."

"So…you're leaving tomorrow? Any particular time?"

"Not really. Whenever I get the last of my stuff tucked into my little car. Maybe around noon."

"Can I take you to breakfast, help you pack…?"

"You know I'd love that, Brett. What about the office?"

"I'll leave a message for Becky that I won't be in till afternoon. Don't have anything on in the morning that I need to worry about. Want to walk?" he asked as they drove along Springbank Park.

"Wonderful idea. And then let's drive through some of the rural areas. I love the orchards, wheat, cattle country."

"So…tell me, Lee…why you're going to Toronto so early. Seems to me the newlyweds won't need the house for a couple more weeks…."

"I did tell you I was going to take a holiday."

"Toronto is a holiday?"

"No. Definitely not. I'm going to visit my aunt and uncle in England; I'll be gone almost two weeks, leaving Wednesday. Aunt Beth is Dad's sister. She came for his funeral and prevailed upon me to come for a visit."

He sat quietly on the bench watching the geese as she continued. "Actually, I hope to spend at least a week just seeing the countryside. I picked up a Britrail pass…feel like I need some time to myself…to sort and sift…find out what's really important to me, before I re-enter the clamour and pressure of U of T."

She found his silence uncomfortable. "Why so quiet? Something you disapprove of?"

"No. Of course not. Just wish we knew each other a little better. Wish I knew…." He broke off, avoiding her gaze.

"…what the future holds?" she guessed.

"Maybe."

"Do we really need to know? Can't we trust God to lead us in the right direction?" She took his hand. "Brett, we'll get to know each other…we just need a little time. I feel like I need a little distance so I can think through some things. I already know you're important to me…that isn't going to change."

He smiled and offered his arm as they resumed their walk. "You're important to me, too, Lee." She noticed that his voice was husky.

"How do you keep so fit?" she asked in an effort to lighten the conversation. Do you swim, roller blade, play racquetball, jog, ski…?

He chuckled. "None of the above at the present time. Used to swim, play racquetball, basketball…never been much of a jogger. I have equipment at home…work out a couple of times a week. Guess I'd like to get back into swimming, and try some skiing. Used to skate a lot when I was a kid. It's a heap more fun if you have a companion…."

"Dave's into all that stuff. He'll need a racquetball partner; Sherry absolutely refuses to play with him…that might give you a clue." She laughed. "Do you still have your skates?"

"No…but if you promise to skate with me, I'll have a pair by fall."

"It's a deal."

"So where are we heading?" he asked as they pulled out of the park.

"What about the area around Kitchener-Waterloo…all those neat Mennonite farms? Do you like St. Jacobs? Maybe I can treat you to supper?"

"It's my treat. Whenever I take my girl out…it's my treat. Remember that, okay?"

He enjoyed her obvious delight at the small shops, homemade candies, unique quilts, the maple-syrup factory, the green-rolling countryside. "I just love to drive through the country," she exclaimed from time to time. "There's always something beautiful in every season in Southwestern Ontario."

"Guess I hadn't seen it quite this way before," he acknowledged. "You're an interesting girl, Lee. You have such a refreshing approach to life. No wonder I enjoy your company so much."

"I enjoy yours, too, Brett. Even if you are a flatterer." She smiled.

"Do you like live theater?"

"Love it."

"Want to go sometime?"

"Love to."

<hr>

"Guess we need to get on the road," he suggested as they sat in the restaurant. "Can't believe it's 9:30. Where did the day go?"

"It gets used up in a hurry when it's with a good friend."

They drove in companionable silence. The night had settled around them and the lights of London twinkled in the distance.

"Wish we could do this every week." He squeezed her hand.

"You'd be tired of me in no time."

"Like to find out for myself." He grinned.

They sat in the car for a few minutes, looking at the house. It had been home to Lee since she was born. After tomorrow it would be home no more. She suddenly felt like weeping…locking herself in…not giving away a part of her heritage. She had been the one to offer her share to Dave and Sherry. It seemed such a right and good thing to do. She wouldn't be here anyway. They needed a home. It was all so logical. But it was a done deal. She now owned a condo in Toronto…lovely though it was…it would never be home.

As though he felt her pain, Brett leaned over and took her in his arms. "What are you thinking, kitten?"

"About tomorrow. About leaving this home for the last time." She burst into tears. "I didn't think it would be so hard when I suggested it to Dave…I was so sure…."

He held her and let her cry. *She really does have a lot of things to think through*, he told himself, and wished desperately he could be of help. Suddenly, he knew where to find help.

"Can I pray for you?" he offered.

She looked up, surprised.

"I can pray, you know. I'm still God's child…I heard the judge say at our prayer group that He never leaves us or forsakes us. So…he never left me after all…when I got so mad at him when I was a kid; I'm still his child."

"Oh, Brett," she said, snuggling into his arms. "Yes, pray for me, please do."

"Dear God," he prayed. "You know how much Lee is hurting right now, and how painful it is for her to leave her home…this place where she grew up. Help her to have peace…and to know that you are always with her, that you will protect and keep her wherever she goes. And Lord…I ask you to give her wisdom in the decisions that she will make this year. Help her…help us…to want your plan rather than our own."

"Thank you." She smiled through her sniffles. "Thank you for understanding…and for praying for me; I really do feel better."

CHAPTER SEVENTEEN

Friday morning, he mused as he headed to the office. *Becky and I have made it right through to Friday. Lee will be in England by now.*

"Morning, Becky."

"Good morning, Mr. Walker." She handed him the morning paper.

He spread it on his desk, already engrossed in the lead article…the horrors of foot-and-mouth disease in England…spreading into France. What a time for Lee to go. He refolded the paper and picked up his coffee mug.

"Where did that come from?" he asked out loud as he noticed the small beautifully wrapped package on his desk. Burgundy and gold…a spray of golden ribbon that reminded him of a waterfall…who in the world…?

"Becky!"

She scurried in. "What is it, Mr. Walker?"

"Where did this come from?"

"Maybe you should open it and see." She left as quickly as she had come.

"Wow," he exclaimed as he opened the small box. "A day minder!"

The card said, "Happy Birthday, Brett. Just a re-minder….*Lee*"

My birthday! How did she know about that? Forgot about it myself. He sat trying to remember how many years it had been since he'd gotten a birthday present…probably ten or twelve.

He started to look through the enclosed information. Obviously, it would hold any amount of data that he would need to enter… addresses…phone and fax numbers…appointments…dates. He chuckled as he saw that she had underlined the low-battery feature. It would beep at intervals of six hours the first two days, then down to three hours, finally to once per hour. She had drawn a smiley face.

She's quite a girl! May as well get on with entering some of this stuff. He turned to the most-used numbers and clicked the data entry. The name and number appeared on the screen. He continued to investigate…all of the law firms he did business with…the Court House, Land Titles Office…Prosecutor's Office…Police Department…long-term clients. He clicked *Stevenson*, and found Dave and Sherry's address and phone number. Scrolling down he found Lee's number in Toronto. He sat back smiling. *The little rascal! She must have spent hours putting this stuff in here.* So she was not intending to forget him. At least she was serious about having him call her.

Well, call her he would…but how to find her in England. Becky…yes Becky would have a number in case she needed help with something. She supplied the number happily, reminding him that England was five hours ahead of Ontario. So…it would be 2:00 p.m. in Bedford.

"Good afternoon, this is the Witherington residence." A very British accent, he noted.

"Leanne," he explained in answer to Brett's query, "and Martyn are touring today. I believe they plan to take in the cinema this evening. They should be in shortly after ten, I should say. Shall I have her call you, Mr. Walker?"

"Would it be too late for me to call by 10:30?"

"Not at all, not at all. If they should stop in before they go to the cinema, I shall tell her to expect your call."

What a gracious man her uncle is. But who, pray tell, is Martyn? So, he could not call until 5:30…a whole day's work to be done before then. He pressed the intercom. "Becky, can you take some dictation?"

Her call came at noon. He was thankful to be alone in the office.

"We stopped in to change before heading to the cinema. Had a great day with my cousin, Martyn. Haven't seen each other for about twelve years…he's changed some…not much!" He could hear her cousin in the background denying, laughing, teasing. "We spent the day at

Warwick Castle; what a lot of history there!" She seemed to be having a good time.

She wished him happy birthday...pleased he liked her gift. She would leave Monday for her trip across northern England, Scotland and Wales. Then stop again with the Witheringtons for a few days before leaving for London and Toronto. She missed him. She would call again from Edinburgh...her uncle had arranged a bed and breakfast there for her. Then she was gone...but her whisper still curled around his heart, "I miss you, too, Brett...so much."

Guess I must be in love, he concluded.

❧

"I am enjoying just being here by myself," she assured him when she called from Wales. "I'm among total strangers on the train...no need for conversation...lots of time to think...work through some things. I did cause quite a stir yesterday, though. Pulled the wrong cord in the bathroom and stopped the mainline express. A bit of excitement there while they decided whether or not to charge me the fifty-pound fine. Finally decided I was a rather dumb tourist."

"I think you need me along to take care of you."

"I'm beginning to think you're right. Wouldn't have helped with the bathroom, though." She laughed. "I take it the newlyweds must be back?"

"Affirmative...and the honeymoon seems to have been more than expected. Not nearly over, apparently. Dave shows up each day with a rose in his lapel, whistling a tune. Sherry comes by every day and they eat lunch together."

"Sounds like Dave and Sherry. She'll be back teaching school pretty soon and will have to forego that little pleasure. They need to enjoy it while they can. Did they tell anyone where they went?"

"The Maritimes. Weather and beaches were great. So when can I expect to meet you in Toronto?"

"Wow! That's sounds like an offer that shouldn't be refused. The flight arrives Saturday morning around 9:00? Isn't that a bit early for a Londoner?"

"Not if you're on it."

"I'll be there."

So will I, he assured himself. *Just five more days....*

Chapter Eighteen

"Is this seat taken? Do you mind if I join you?"

He looked up from the paper he was enjoying over lunch in Tim Horton's. "By all means," he offered, folding the paper. His eyes took in her curves…plunging neckline, too-short, too-tight leather skirt. Her long blonde hair hung about her shoulders as if to cover her nakedness.

"You're the lawyer from down the hall, aren't you? Brett Walker, isn't it?" Her eyes travelled slowly appraising his physique; she smiled as she noticed his slight blush.

"So you must be the new student—articling with Hansen?" She seemed pleasant enough.

"Yes…yes…I'm Rhonda Fleming." She extended her hand.

"Well, I'm pleased to meet you, Miss Fleming…Rhonda. Guess we'll see you in the course of duty." He rose to go.

"So we shall…so we shall!" She smiled again. *A whole lot more than you know, big boy,* she mused as the door closed behind him.

He could hear Sherry and Dave chuckling in the lunch room as he made his way to his office. *Just a couple more days,* he told himself, *and I'll be chuckling, too.*

❧

"Brett Walker," she said as she slid into the seat opposite him. "Imagine that, two days in a row. How lucky can a girl get!"

He had to admit she was attractive as she leaned forward and smiled up into his face several times. Her bright chatter certainly added a little spice to an otherwise drab lunch hour.

"Could I stop by and see you about a small matter that's been troubling me?" she asked as he rose to go. "Would appreciate someone outside the firm…you know…hate to have my private affairs circulating among six lawyers."

"Give Becky a call; she'll arrange something."

"He was surprised when Becky showed her in several hours later. Even more surprised when the advice she sought could best be handled by an insurance agent—something about liability insurance on a cabin her father owned at Port Franks…and a gathering of friends over the Thanksgiving weekend. *Funny*, he mused, *that a law student wouldn't know any better than that!* He shrugged his shoulders as he went back to a busy afternoon.

"Was that Rhonda Fleming?" Dave asked with a note of incredulity.

"Yeah, she's articling with the Hansen group. Wanted to see someone about a little insurance matter. Sent her to an agent."

"Well, I'll be," Dave said as he shook his head. "Well, I'll be!" Then placing a file on Brett's desk, he continued, "I've been going over the boys' files…excellent records. Don't know why we couldn't ask for suspended sentences on all three."

They spent the next hour going over the information and setting out a strategy for the trial, which would be coming up in a few weeks.

"What are you hearing from Lee?" Dave asked as he rose to go.

"Meeting her at Pearson on Saturday morning."

"Bringing her home?"

"Sure would like to. I could take her back Sunday afternoon."

"Great! She needs to come home at least once before she hits the books," Dave said as he headed back to his office, but his smile belied the nagging suspicion at the corner of his mind. *So Rhonda is after Brett!*

❦

His heart skipped a beat as he saw her make her way through Customs, then watched her face light up as she spied him on the other side of the glass doors.

Then she was in his arms—luggage scattered at her feet.

"Kitten," he said between kisses. "Will you come to London with me…Dave and Sherry's for supper? I could bring you back tomorrow."

She nodded into his shoulder. "Whatever you've arranged will be just fine. Let's just spend it together."

She was warmer, friendlier, cuddlier than he'd remembered. And more kissable! *This holiday has been good for her*, he decided. He could hardly wait to hear all the details.

She wanted to know all about the office, and how he and Becky were coping; he happily filled her in as they sped swiftly along the 401.

Dave and Sherry's house was a beehive as family and friends came to say hello and stopped to eat and visit with Lee. "Sunday dinner is my treat," she announced, "and don't you prepare anything, Sherry. Time you relaxed a little. We've hardly seen each other. There's a neat smorg at The Steak House; I'll reserve for the four of us after church."

❦

"Well, this weekend has just evaporated," he commented as they headed back to the 401. "And I haven't heard nearly enough about your trip and how your time went in Britain. Guess we just spent too much time visiting."

"I did some real soul searching. Think I got my priorities in order. I really need to tell you about it…maybe we'll talk about it sometime…soon. But it was really good to see Dave and Sherry again. Thanks for being so gracious this weekend." She paused, then added, "I'm glad to be back; I really missed you, Brett."

His thoughts lingered on their goodnight kiss; she was warm and responsive…her perfume faint and elusive…her arms around his neck. She was his kitten…all he had dreamed of…and more. He would see her again in a few weeks. Time to tell her he loved her; time to get serious, he decided.

"Brett Walker, I dare say you're following me," she said as she slipped her long legs into the seat beside him at Wendy's."

"I dare say *you're* following *me*, Rhonda," he commented as she leaned closer to read his paper.

She laughed up at him with a twinkle in her eyes. "What's a girl to do with a tiger like you running loose…and just down the hall? Honestly, Brett…."

It was time to leave, except that her presence blocked him in.

She chuckled. "Not so fast, not so fast. What's the matter? Don't you know that rushing is bad for the digestion and a whole lot of other things?" She winked. "Besides, I have a couple of things I need to run by you."

"I'm sure your six-pack can handle it," he smirked, referring to the law firm. "Now if you'll excuse me," he rose as he spoke and she found it necessary to make way for him.

"Really, Brett…this is nothing they would be concerned with…this is quite personal…." She looked at him pleadingly.

He was forced to brush against her on his way out of the booth. "Give my secretary a call," he suggested. "She might be able to work you in next week." *Little wretch*, he muttered on his way back to the office. *She knows all the angles.*

The two men looked up in surprise as she burst into Brett's office unannounced.

"Really, Brett, you know how upset…." She stopped as she saw Dave.

"I didn't realize you had an appointment with me," he said. "Did Becky…?"

"Of course not. It's after five."

"I did suggest you get an appointment. As you can see, we're extremely busy and will be for some time. I don't take appointments after five."

"Honestly, Brett. You can be so harsh!" She backed off like a hurt child, leaving the impression of an intimate relationship.

It was not lost on Dave. He looked questioningly at Brett.

"Don't know what's gotten into her; she's got six lawyers to choose from," Brett muttered as he went back to the subject at hand.

"Thanks for coming today, Brett. I have so enjoyed having you all to myself…all day. So, I'll see you at Uncle Ben's for Thanksgiving?" she asked as they pulled up to her door.

He was quiet for a moment, then asked, "Is that important to you, Lee…that I be there?"

"Why? Got other plans?"

"Don't know. Thinking about it."

She raised an eyebrow, waiting.

"Lee, there is something I need to tell you. I have been seeing someone else these last few weeks, and she's invited me to her cottage…."

She sat stunned. "You're dating someone else?" she asked, her voice almost a whisper.

"Well, I haven't actually dated her, but she'd sure like me to…. She's joined me for lunch a number of times, and…and she's come to the office for advice. I haven't really dated her…but…."

"But you'd like to?" she whispered.

"Don't know. Guess I'd like to be free to decide. How would you feel if I did?"

"Oh, Brett…Brett," was all she could manage as her voice caught.

"I didn't tell her I would go. At first I thought she was inviting both of us…she says she knows you…but then…."

"Knows me? Who are we talking about?"

"She's the student articling with Hansen; her name is Rhonda Fleming."

"Rhonda Fleming!" She bolted upright. "You're dating Rhonda?…Fleming?"

"Stop it, Lee." His voice had that familiar edge. "Are you saying I can't?"

"No. No. Of course not. But Rhonda Fleming?"

"So you're angry? Jealous?"

She tried to look at him but her eyes filled with tears. She moved to open the door, but he caught her hand.

"What is it, Lee? Why won't you discuss this with me? Why can't we be a little more adult? Are you trying to manipulate me?"

"Oh, Brett," she whispered through her tears. "Oh, Brett."

"I'm sorry, Lee. Guess I should have left this till later. You were going to tell me about the decisions you made while you were in England. Can we salvage an hour and…?"

She sat…her emotions numb…*Rhonda…Rhonda Fleming…Oh God, help him!*

"You'd better go, Brett," she managed at last. "Any decisions I made back then were made on insufficient information…and…and the little I had…I seem to have misinterpreted," she finished in a whisper. The car door yielded and she stumbled up the steps.

"Lee…kitten," he said as he tried to take her key to unlock the door. "Can we get together after Thanksgiving and discuss this a little more rationally?"

"Brett," she said, suddenly finding her voice, "when Rhonda is through with you…." She stepped inside and shut the door.

He tried to call her several times on the cell phone as he sat on the driveway. The house remained dark and silent.

CHAPTER NINETEEN

He was angry as he eased into the traffic on the 401. He had not expected Lee's reaction. After all, she knew Rhonda. She didn't even give him a chance to tell her that he was only helping her out for the weekend because her boyfriend had stood her up. Maybe he shouldn't have told her...at least not yet. Still a week before then. *Funny*, he thought, *she didn't really get upset until I told her it was Rhonda. And that parting missile she fired...'when Rhonda gets through with you....' That's pretty vindictive...wouldn't have thought it of Lee...unless...of course...she knows something I don't.*

He pondered that as he drove. There was that look on Dave's face...and the look on Rhonda's when she found out Dave was articling with him. Something going on there! He would need to find out before he went for the weekend. He wished Lee would have been more up front with him...course he may not have believed her. Anyway, she was too upset. He hated that he had upset her. She was precious to him. When he got this thing over with and decided what to do with Rhonda...? Who could he go to for advice? Dave? But Dave didn't like her. Maybe he needed to find out why.

He dreamed in fits and starts. He was dancing with Lee, holding her close as she snuggled into his shoulder...his neck. She lifted her lips for his kiss...and suddenly she was Rhonda...tempting...laughing up at him. *Oh, God*, he prayed, as he wiped the sweat from his face, *show me what to do.* "Guess I'm a little late; should have asked that a long time ago," he said aloud.

He dozed, only to wake trembling…clutching the bedding…the pillow over his head. He was a small boy again…terrified…hiding. The dream was coming more often, leaving him exhausted and frightened. Perhaps he needed help; he assured himself he would go if this persisted, but right now he had way too much on his plate….

She sat in the chair where she had collapsed when she came in…her head in her hands. Her sobs had ceased now…just dry heaves escaped her trembling body. Until now, she had been so sure that Brett was a part of the plan God had for her life. Now she prayed over and over. "Oh, God…oh, God." She had long since lost track of time. "Please God," she finally managed, "don't let her destroy him…he's your child…protect him."

Thoughts…questions crowded into her mind…why hadn't he told her about this when he came? They had enjoyed such a special day— talking, laughing, holding each other. His kisses…. She'd had no warning that he was seeing someone else. *Rhonda*…the very name sent her into despair. And she had been all excited to tell him how she felt about him…nothing to tell now…just *numb*! One thing was for sure…she couldn't face her family on Thanksgiving…Dave and Sherry would question Brett's absence; they would feel sorry for her. No. Better she should accept the invitation to go on the colour tour with her study group. Two couples and herself; they would spend a couple nights in a cabin in cottage country. It would get her through the weekend…better than crying at home alone, she decided.

Meantime…she forced her mind into more profitable channels; she had tomorrow to think about…and that meeting with Lonnie Hencken. One more thing she had planned to discuss with Brett! *Can't imagine why Lonnie thinks I'm doing so badly in his Advocacy class. Something going on here…can't imagine one more crisis in my life right now.* Suddenly feeling all alone in the world, she sobbed, *Oh, God, I need help!*

She glanced at the clock. It was long past midnight…not that she'd sleep much anyway.

I need some comfort, Lord, need to feel you close to me. She opened her Bible to her favourite Psalm…139:

> *O Lord, you have searched me and you know me,*
> *You know when I sit and when I rise;*
> *You perceive my thoughts from afar.*
> *You discern my going out and my lying down;*
> *You are familiar with all my ways.*
> *Before a word is on my tongue you know it completely, O Lord.*

"Thank you, God," she whispered as she continued:

> *You hem me in—behind and before; you have laid your hand upon me.*
> *Such knowledge is too wonderful for me, too lofty for me to attain.*
> *Where can I go from your Spirit? Where can I flee from your presence?*
> *If I go up to the heavens, you are there;*
> *if I make my bed in the depths, you are there.*
> *If I rise on the wings of the dawn, if I settle on the far side of the sea,*
> *even there your hand will guide me, your right hand will hold me fast.*
> Ps. 139:1-10 NIV

Yes, Lord, You know me intimately; You will guide me, and your right hand will hold me fast, she reminded herself as she slowly drifted into a deep sleep.

He was glad that Dave wasn't in yet. Maybe a black coffee would ease his throbbing head and help him decide how to approach the delicate matter before him. He'd have to make the coffee himself;

101

Becky wouldn't be in for another half hour. Probably Dave wouldn't either—he may have stopped at Tim's to pick up an early coffee.

"Brett! What is going on here?" The young man towered over his desk, his eyes ablaze.

"Going on where?" he had never seen Dave so angry.

"With that…that…that…law student from down the hall?"

"So you've been talking to Lee?"

"I haven't talked to Lee. Didn't know she knew about this. I just came from Tim Horton's. You seem to be the talk of the coffee shop. A whole group of young gals—who obviously didn't know who I was—laughing up a storm. 'Rhonda's latest conquest…and Brett Walker at that! Goes to show you…even the tough guys can't stand up to Rhonnie. She'll fix him good. She sure did that Jamieson in….' and on and on. So, you're going on a weekend with this…this….!"

"Just hold it right there. You have no call to talk to me like that." He stopped, surprised at the anger in his voice—at the anger in Dave. They had never addressed each other like this before.

"You're right, Brett. I apologize. I have no right to interfere in your private life. I am concerned for you…." He hesitated. "I guess I thought that you and Lee…I want you to leave her alone, Brett. She thinks you're…well, she doesn't know you very well…guess I don't either…she's not like you. *Leave her alone!*" he finished emphatically.

The lawyer sat in a daze. So his law student was now giving directives. What an interesting turn of events. How unlike Dave to forget his place in the scheme of things.

Dave read his thoughts. "I'm prepared to resign, Brett," he offered. "But I won't have you toying with my sister."

"Do you always condemn without a trial?"

From two Stevensons down to none…all in twelve hours! How in the world did I get myself into this? And what do they know that I don't?

"Dave," he said angrily, "either sit down and tell me what's on your mind, or shut up and get out of my office."

"Which do you really want me to do, Brett?"

He motioned toward the chair. "SIT!"

"What do you want to know?"

"Tell me what you know about Rhonda."

"Same as everybody else. Why are you asking?"

"Because I don't seem to be a part of the *everybody else*."

"Forever more! Where've you been?"

"Never mind that. I never heard of her before she came to the Hansen Group. How long have you known her? Start there."

"Lee met her at UWO when she started taking night classes after Mom's death. She was pregnant and distressed. Lee offered to help…brought her home to stay with us. She tried to make out with me…ran around in an open bathrobe and little else. We offered to help her through the pregnancy and adopt out the baby. She chuckled. Took off for a few days and showed up all white and shaky; she'd had it aborted. It was hard having her around; her smoking really bothered Dad, but she didn't worry about that. She came home one night with a guy…both of them high on something. We wouldn't let him spend the night with her. She was furious…called us down before they left for the night; never heard such language in my entire life! Lee made her leave the next day. She continued her tirade and threatened to get even.

"She told Lee her dad gave her everything she ever wanted while she was growing up…after she gave him everything he wanted. Said she didn't choose her classes by content…but by professor.

"She has a reputation for destroying men…guess she's getting even with her dad. She gets a party going at his cabin at Port Franks…."

"Do you have evidence to support this kind of accusation?"

Dave sat staring at his boss, wondering if he was really that naive, or just playing dumb. "Do you know Roger Jamieson?"

"Of course. What's he got to do with this? He's got enough problems of his own."

"'What's *she* got to do with this?' you mean. He told me his second marriage was really doing quite well until they had a spat one night and his wife locked the bedroom door. He was so ticked off he decided to teach her a lesson; accepted the oft-repeated invite to Rhonda's weekend bash. He's an admitted womanizer, but not much of a drinker. However, as he tells it, his first drink was laced with something. He didn't come to until sometime Sunday afternoon. He hadn't intended to spend the night…just give his wife a good scare. Rhonda apparently has a camera-happy *friend* that does her bidding and the evidence he compiled over the weekend was pretty convicting. She intended to use it. The friend now became jealous, and upped his price for the snapshots. She wouldn't give. He took them to Roger. Roger beat him up and took them away. He made more and gave them to Roger's wife. End of marriage number two. Rhonda laughing it up in the coffee shops."

"She does seem to enjoy meeting me in the coffee shops. I swear she keeps track of me; how else would she know where I'm going?"

"That's how she gets the rumour mill started. Then she tells someone…whom she is sure will tell someone else. Then they see her there with her victim. She told Lee all about it. When she doesn't get her way, she cries. She can turn it on in a second…first her bottom lip comes out like a petulant two-year-old, then the tears. She showed us one night…when she was done, she burst out laughing and walked away. She's a very troubled woman…needs help desperately…but she has a mind like a criminal…. Keep out of her way."

Brett's anger at Dave had evaporated. "So you think I knew all this and was going to go with her anyway?"

"Guess I thought everybody knew about the Roger thing. She spread it far and wide—taking full credit for the marriage break-up."

"If that's all true, why didn't he charge her?"

"Don't know. Didn't ask. Probably didn't want the world to know he'd spent the weekend with her."

"So you think this is more than a few friends getting together for a house party?"

"Look at her and you'll have your answer to that. Besides, she's been seen with you so often in the last few weeks…."

"Rumour mill already producing!"

"No joke. Look what I heard this morning. You're all set up for the big time."

They sat quietly for a few minutes, each busy with his own thoughts.

"How do you think you got into this?" Dave asked at last. "What made you susceptible to this kind of a woman?"

"Susceptible is far too strong, but I did ask myself that last night on the way home from Toronto. Don't really know…never been overly attracted to women…guess I just numbed out my emotions…until I got to know Lee. I fell for her—big time! Guess when I opened up my emotions to her…. I don't know. I'm guessing. Trying to make sense out of this stupidity. Then last night when I couldn't sleep, I started to pray. Asked God to give me wisdom—guess he just answered that one. But it made me see some things…I really don't know God; I know I'm one of His, but I don't know His Word, His ways, what He wants me to do…that sort of thing."

"Do you read your Bible?"

"Don't have one, but I'll correct that. Guess I need some sort of a guide to tell me how to study…."

"Honestly, Brett…you are so elusive." She came through the door unannounced in her usual style, and stopped abruptly as she saw Dave.

"Good morning, Rhonda," he offered.

"Good morning, Dave. I have a little business to attend to with Brett," she said as she dismissed him.

"Me, too," Dave countered, "and I got here first."

She looked appealingly at Brett.

"What would you like, Rhonda?"

"How about a private word for starters."

"Sorry! Dave and I were just in the middle of a very important discussion. You and I have nothing private to discuss…nothing Dave can't be privy to."

"Honestly, Brett. You can be so harsh." Her bottom lip came out, and tears filled her blue-shadowed eyes. "You know I can't speak my thoughts to just anybody."

"I should mention, Rhonda, that I won't be coming to your party on the weekend."

"Why is that?" She looked accusingly at Dave.

"Because I have decided not to."

"But why…why would you ruin…?" More tears.

He sat watching her performance—annoyed and amused by turns. "Because I have some things I would rather do. Sorry, but I did tell you

I would need time to think it over. I have thought it over. I won't be there."

"Perhaps we can discuss this again…in more private circumstances." She gave him a pitiful smile as she headed for the door.

"End of Act One," Dave smirked.

"That was quite the performance. Thanks for cluing me in."

"I'd best get on with…."

"Can you sit for a few more minutes, Dave? I know the timing is bad…but you must know that I don't want you to abort your articles here. In fact, I was hoping we might talk partnership…I know it's early to be thinking about it, but if I know Foster…he won't be shy in getting a proposal…."

"He's way ahead of you, Brett."

"Meaning?"

"Got an offer weeks ago."

The lawyer sat silently, his heart heavy. "You never mentioned it. Guess I won't be able to compete with what he can offer."

"No need to mention it…or to compete. I haven't been looking for another job; in fact I was hoping we might be able to go on working together. Never really thought otherwise…until this morning…I wouldn't be able to deal with the Rhonda thing…especially if you were still seeing Lee. She's mine to protect, you know…until she marries."

Again he sat silently. "What does that mean…in terms that a very tired and confused lawyer can understand? Do I take it you're interested in staying on…provided Rhonda isn't around?"

He nodded. "I'd really appreciate the opportunity to go on working with you, Brett."

"Thanks, pal. Me, too. What does that mean where Lee is concerned?"

Dave looked at him for a long moment.

"I'm not guilty, you know. I've never touched this woman…through no fault of hers!"

"I believe you, buddy, but I wonder how a guy can trade in Lee…for…for…."

"Didn't intend it to go that way. She just got so upset when I mentioned Rhonda…I'm not even sure she'll consider…."

Chapter Twenty

Lee prepared for her meeting with Lonnie Hencken with trepidation. If the things she heard from the other girls were true, she would have to do more than study to get a pass in his class. She shuddered as his image flashed through her mind...his thinning grey-blonde hair, pointed nose and chin, sunken eyes, high cheek bones...bony fingers always fidgeting nervously here and there.

Please, God, help me to do what is right. Give me wisdom to know who to go to with this...if I have an ally somewhere. Suddenly, she knew what to do—go to the dean of the faculty. Would he be sympathetic? He'd certainly need evidence...not a lot of innuendos and accusations. *Maybe I need to tape this conversation...my little tape recorder...haven't seen it since I moved...must be here somewhere...yes...yes...in my desk drawer...I'm sure I saw it there...and batteries...yes.... What if I put this in my computer case...it would be a natural thing to place it on his desk when I arrive. It used to pick up really well.* She smiled as she recalled some of Dave's shenanigans.

❧

"Good morning, Lee." The professor greeted her warmly.

"Good morning, Mr. Hencken."

"*Lonnie...*remember? *Mr. Hencken* is far too formal for such good friends."

"You wanted to discuss my progress?"

"Yes, yes, Lee. I hate to have to bring this to your attention…but you really don't seem to be getting the intent and purpose of the class…." He paused and waited for her reaction.

"Can you be a little more specific? I'm not sure what I need to do to improve."

"Well, it can be quite illusive. I often find that bright students like yourself are the ones who stumble the most in my class. While I can't give special attention to all of them, I do try to be of special encouragement to those I feel might make their mark in life. You definitely are in that category…Lee." Again, he paused and smiled, and waited for her reaction.

"I have been trying very hard to follow your directives, Mr. Hencken; I really am prepared to work at it, if I can just get a handle on what it is I'm missing."

She despised the ingratiating way he smiled at her. *Must think I'm an idiot*, she mused.

"My dear Lee." He reached for her hand across the desk. "Why don't we discuss this when we have a little more time. Rushing like this between classes just isn't going to do it justice. Now let me see…." He opened his day minder and made small clucking noises as he purported to look for just the right time. "Not much available during the day. Evening?…a possibility. Would you be free tomorrow evening?"

He had caught her off guard. She hadn't prepared for this. What to do? What to do? Pray, of course. *Oh, God, help.*

"Actually, Mr. Hencken, my evenings are pretty full this week. My study groups meets several times; I'm trying to finish some major papers."

"It's Lonnie, remember. And really, Lee, are you saying that you don't have the time to put into my course? You do have to pass it to graduate, you know…." He left the sentence hanging.

"I appreciate that, Lonnie, and I appreciate your willingness to help. It's just that I do have time during the day…two hours this afternoon…."

"But I don't, of course, Lee. You can hardly expect a professor to accommodate himself to your schedule. If I did that for every student…."

ing—ing——ing—

"Of course, I'm sorry. I know I can't possibly make it tomorrow evening; perhaps a little later in the week."

Again the clucking and the clicking of the day minder. "Shall we say Thursday then?"

She nodded numbly. "I'll do my best." *Oh, Lee, what have you gotten yourself into?*

"Can I meet you somewhere?" she asked as she rose to go.

"That will hardly be necessary. I still know how to treat a lady. Your address is…ah, yes, here it is. Shall we say around seven? You may want to wear something…dressy. Education needn't be dowdy."

The portly, grey-haired gentleman rose, smiling warmly as he extended his hand.

"Good afternoon, Dean Strauss, I'm Leanne Stevenson, senior law student."

"Yes…you are indeed! I've been following your progress. I was saddened to hear that you dropped out of our program a year or two ago. What brings you back?"

She was taken aback at his knowledge of her. "I dropped out to care for my father, following my mother's death. He was injured badly as well, and passed away in March. I was able to take a few night classes at UWO."

"Yes, yes, I knew your father well. A good friend! A good friend! I was sorry…very sorry indeed to hear of his passing. But we're glad you're back, Leanne. Enjoyed having your brother. Understand he's articling with Brett Walker. They should make a good team!"

"Yes, they do. They quite enjoy working together. A good match."

"Now, Miss Leanne, what brings you to the dean's office?"

Oh, God, it's Lee again. Help! "I'm really not sure I'm in the right place; perhaps you could direct me if I'm not. I seem to be having some difficulty with one of my profs. He insists I'm doing badly in his course…yet won't give me the direction he says I need. He has mentioned a couple of times that I do need to pass his course in order to graduate."

He listened quietly, nodding occasionally.

"I'm sorry," she stammered. "Maybe I just need to figure this out by myself…I'm sorry to have taken your time…."

"Not at all…not at all. Carry on with your story. Perhaps you might tell me which class you are struggling with."

"Strangely enough its *Advocacy*. I thought it was really one of my best subjects. I'm really at a loss…."

"So your professor is Mr. Hencken?" he asked without bothering to check the record. "You are not alone; others have struggled with this course. Tell me…what advice has Mr. Hencken offered?"

"There seems to be…I'm not sure. I…I'm not sure I did a good thing…but I taped our last conversation."

"Do you have it with you?"

She nodded.

"Shall we hear it, then?"

She pulled the small recorder from her bag and turned it on. The dean's face remained passive as he listened.

"Are you comfortable in leaving this with me?" he asked.

She hesitated. Clearly she was not. She had kept a copy but…what would the dean do with it? Could she trust him?

As if reading her thoughts, he assured her, "You can trust me with this, Leanne. And with anything else you choose to record. Do you intend to go on Thursday evening?"

"I would prefer not. Don't know what else to do."

"If you go, I suggest you meet him there. Call him from somewhere at the last hour and insist. That will give you an out if you are feeling threatened."

"Thank you for your support, Mr. Strauss. I am…."

"Relieved," he finished for her. "Keep in touch with me, Leanne. I shall be watching this very carefully. And don't worry about your grades; he wouldn't dare fail a student of your calibre. It would be best if you didn't share this with anyone."

She nodded. *They know about this guy. Sounds like they just need some hard evidence to nail him. Wish Susan and Kim had told me their stories sooner. Wonder if they'll be willing to share them with the dean.*

☙✷❧

He picked up the package left on his desk over the lunch hour. *Wow! New International Version of the Bible…deep rich brown, genuine leather. Bible Study Guide. Only one person could have put it there.*

He crossed the hall to Dave's office.

"Sorry, Mr. Walker. Mr. Stevenson won't be in till around three."

He smiled and retreated to his desk. Then he would just take time to check out this incredible gift. He turned to the first chapter of Genesis; time slipped away as he became absorbed in the mysteries of creation.

"For heaven's sake, Brett, what are you doing? Is it any wonder you're so messed up?"

"Hello, Rhonda. I thought we settled our business this morning."

"What do you mean by that? What kind of a man are you anyway…afraid of a little honest fun? Hiding behind this religious stuff…I suppose Dave got you into that hocus pocus…really, Brett…for a while there I thought you might be the real thing…."

"That will do, Rhonda. You got my answer this morning and, as you can see, I am quite occupied."

"You don't dismiss me that easy, big boy," she said, perching on the corner of his desk and crossing her long, bare legs. "I have a little something owing…and I aim to collect." She produced a snapshot of herself and Brett behind the newspaper in Wendy's.

So her friend was at work that day, too. He glanced carelessly at the photo, noting that his face was indiscernible, then remarked, "Since you have finished your business, Rhonda, I would bid you a good day."

She laughed arrogantly. "Not quite so fast; I have more where this came from. Now do we have a deal?"

He touched the programmed number on his desk phone. "Hansen," he roared, "get your law student out of my office, and keep her out of here before I get a restraining order."

111

He had pulled the rug from under her. She scrambled to her feet. Then turning to him once more she squinted her eyes and pointed one long bronze nail in his direction. "You will be sorry, Brett Walker. You haven't heard the last of this. You'll find out who you're dealing with."

"I just have," he muttered as the door closed behind her.

CHAPTER TWENTY-ONE

"Mr. Hencken, hello, it's Lee. I'm running quite late today. Met a friend in Cambridge and I'm afraid I'll be fairly pushed for time. Can I meet you at the restaurant?"

"Now, Lee, we had an agreement...your house at seven."

"I won't be there, Mr. Hencken. I'm coming directly from Cambridge; I can meet you at the restaurant by 7:30."

He finally agreed...finding himself frustrated and furious. *How dare she do this to him! This evening would cost him plenty...especially if he could interest her in a few cocktails...and he wanted his money's worth. He hoped she would at least be dressed appropriately.*

She smiled as she made her way through the traffic. Her new recording gadget was safely secured inside her dress. The salesman had assured her it would pick up the faintest whisper. She hoped her dress would meet with his approval...not too low cut in front...but a lovely scoop at the back. Too bad it would be wasted on Lonnie...now if it were Brett! She pushed his image out of her mind...no time to get emotional. She was a woman on a mission.

He met her in the foyer. His glance showed approval. "My dear little Lee, you are a beautiful woman! Shall we go?" he asked as he took her elbow and guided her into the restaurant.

She tried not to recoil as his clammy hand touched her flesh.

He's done his homework, she thought as the hostess showed them to a secluded booth, with ferns and small twinkling lights. *If only this were Brett!* He was dressed as smartly as she had ever seen him...a dark dinner suit...cost him a few shekels, she decided.

He was visibly irritated when she declined the cocktail.

"Perhaps a bottle of dinner wine for the lady?" the waiter suggested. He ordered without asking her permission.

"Really, my dear, you must not be so standoffish. No wonder you are struggling with my class; your relational skills really do need some attention." He smiled in his most ingratiating manner, as he reached across the table and took her hand. "But we'll work on that, won't we?"

She looked at him questioningly.

"Well, we do have the entire evening, don't we, my dear?"

"I am sorry, Mr. Hencken. I must tell you that I have a friend coming to town this evening. I will need to go to the airport; flight arrives around 10:30. Perhaps it would be good if we were to discuss ways…."

"My! My! My! You certainly have a one-track mind. My dear, Miss Lee, I am certainly disappointed in your aborting our time together. I had quite a different evening planned. Surely we can enjoy supper without talking shop. Your course work is in my car; we could more easily discuss it at your place…or perhaps at mine…later this evening. Now, you simply need to call someone to meet your friend, or I can call someone…."

"I am sorry, Mr. Hencken. I had no idea what you had in mind. I am disappointed, too, that I will spend an entire evening without accomplishing what I came for."

He was obviously outraged. *I'm not exactly getting what I came for, either,* he told himself indignantly.

"You are a most ungracious young lady. You can hardly develop relational skills in a couple of hours. Relationship is a ongoing, prolonged…."

"Mr. Hencken, if I can't get a handle on it before ten o'clock, it seems unlikely that it will happen. I need to pick up a friend. I really do have friends…and I don't have a great deal of difficulty relating…." She stopped, suddenly remembering her last evening with Brett.

"There, there my dear. No need to get rattled. I was rather hoping that we might discuss an on-going relationship. I was about to offer you a chance to article with Hencken, Hencken and Mears. It goes without saying that you will need to pass my course. Advocacy is important in our firm. You will need to graduate...at the top of your class...." His voice trailed off, his eyes searched her face, watching for effect. "We don't take just anyone...we are elite as law firms go...on Bay Street...known for only the highest quality in staff...performance...." He rattled on as her mind busily tried to plan her next move. "So, do we have a deal?"

She came to, suddenly realizing he had been prattling while her mind was busy elsewhere. "A deal?" she asked.

"Let's not play games, Leanne. We both know what this evening is all about. Now you will need to call your friend and have her take a taxi. You and I have work to do. You know your career depends on it."

"I'm sorry, Mr. Hencken...." He glared at her and she quickly corrected herself. "Lonnie. I'm sorry you are so disappointed. Perhaps if you had been a little more up front with me...a little more honest about this evening...we both could have been spared a great deal of angst."

Obviously he would not get anywhere tonight; her mind and schedule were full of plans. He would have to take another approach...get her alone where she couldn't run when she felt so inclined. "I am sorry, too, Leanne," he began apologetically; "sorry I didn't make my expectations clear. Now that you realize that this will take time, perhaps we could talk about the long weekend. Cottage country is beautiful at this time of year...my cabin is secluded...quiet...we would be undisturbed."

Noting the look of surprise on her face, he soothed, "Of course, we would have a number of others joining us...perhaps your study group...."

Oh, God, she breathed. *Help.* "Really, Lonnie, Thanksgiving has always been a family time at our house, but this year I have broken with tradition and have arranged a special time with friends."

"Perhaps another weekend." He slipped his day minder from his inner pocket and began his clucking and clicking exercise.

God, I'm still here. She well knew that any escape would need to leave the door open for civility in the classroom. Suddenly her cell phone buzzed loudly. She reached for her small beaded bag and extracted it.

The look on his face was one of utter exasperation…betrayal. This girl had more tricks up her sleeve than he would have thought. She was no innocent student. Well, he was a lawyer…experienced in these matters; he had a few things to show her that she hadn't thought of yet.

"I am sorry, Dave. Actually, I'm quite occupied right now, and I have to pick Bill up at the airport around 10:30. It will be a bit late before I get home. Can I call you tomorrow?"

He made no effort to hide his displeasure. "Frankly, Leanne, I'm disappointed in you. Do you always carry that thing? Allow it to interrupt intimate fellowship? No wonder you have problems relating."

"Not really. It was necessary this evening. My friend thought he might catch an earlier flight. Perhaps I should go, Mr. Hencken. It's nearly ten, and…."

"By all means." He tried to salvage what was left of a tattered evening. He would plan better next time…get her where he wanted her…the little wretch!

CHAPTER TWENTY-TWO

"Brett Walker." He recognized the voice of his old sparring partner, Sergeant Barker.

"Good morning, George, what can I do for you?"

"You can get yourself down here for starters."

"Something on your mind? How about right after lunch? I have a few things…."

"Get your butt down here, Walker. You're being charged with assault. You can come or I will!"

The lawyer sat in stunned silence for a moment, then asked, "And who, pray tell, did I assault?"

"Ms. Rhonda Fleming."

"Well, I'll be…and what, may I ask, did I do to her?"

"Get down here, Walker. I'll ask the questions."

Hope he did a good job, whoever did it, he mused as he headed toward the OPP Station.

"…you do understand that anything you say can be held against you…" the officer finished.

"Of course I do, and I also understand that I'm entitled to counsel. I need to make a phone call." He hoped Dave would have arrived at the office by now.

He dialled quickly and in a few minutes Dave swung through the door.

"And the charge against my client is…?" Dave began.

"Aggravated assault, Section 268 (1) of the Criminal Code."

"And it states?" Dave probed.

"Every one commits an aggravated assault who wounds, maims, disfigures or endangers the life of the complainant. And," the officer added, "every one who commits an aggravated assault is guilty of an indictable offense and liable to imprisonment for a term not exceeding fourteen years."

"And may I ask the nature of this assault and when it is alleged to have occurred?"

"The nature was of such severity as to hospitalize the complainant…a broken arm, dislocated shoulder, blackened eye, possible broken nose. As to the time of occurrence, perhaps Mr. Walker would like to give us a run-down of his activities this weekend, beginning on Friday evening." Brett noticed the look of smug enjoyment as he delivered the request.

"Friday evening," Brett began, "from about 7:00 till 9:00 or 9:30 I was at the jail, spending time with Tony Cortez. The warden should be able to verify that. Saturday morning…well I slept in and just stayed home and read."

"Anybody that can corroborate that story?"

"The cleaning lady came around 9:30 and left around 11:30. Saturday afternoon, I spent on the golf course with Dave, here. Didn't get through till around 8:00. Picked up Dave's wife and went out for supper."

"Come on, come on…get on with it."

"Sunday morning I was in church from 10:00 till 12:00. Thanksgiving Dinner with Judge and Mrs. Ben Davis. Didn't leave for home till sometime after 8:00 p.m."

"Monday?"

"Monday morning…guess that's yesterday…had a late brunch with Dave and Sherry, visited till around 2:00, then left for Toronto."

"What did you do there? Do you have witnesses?"

"Not really. But I might have evidence that I was on my way there. I tried to call Leanne Stevenson. I knew she was away for the weekend but thought she might be back by early evening. I called her number a half dozen times—at least three while I was on the way and three or four while I waited for her. I left messages on her machine; if she hasn't cancelled them by now...."

"Want to check that out?" The officer turned to Dave.

"Hi, Leanne, it's Dave, and I'm at the OPP Station here in London. Have you erased your phone messages since yesterday?"

"No. I got in really late last night; haven't even had time to listen to them."

"Can I ask for your access number? Do you mind? I can explain later."

Quickly he dialled the number and the contents of her answering machine spilled out in the small office.

The lawyers exchanged glances as the messages from Brett were interspersed with messages from Lonnie Hencken.

"Must be a pretty popular little lady, having two suitors after her in one weekend. What was she...gone with a third?" The officer laughed.

Brett had stated the time of each of his calls...three on the way to Toronto...three while he waited for her. His final call was at 9:30 when he left for home. She had not arrived.

"So how do I know you placed these calls when you said you did?"

"They're all interspersed with the calls from Mr. Hencken. He was pretty emphatic about the times he called. Of course you can always call Bell Canada...."

"All right! All right! I'm going to let you go for now. I'll be in touch."

"Can I ask what time this alleged assault took place, and where?" Brett asked.

"Monday evening in her cabin at Port Franks."

"And when and where was she admitted to hospital?" Dave probed.

"Arrived at the emergency in London around 11:00 p.m."

"So my client is absolved of any involvement. He couldn't possibly have left Toronto at 9:30 and driven to Port Franks. I would ask that the charges be dropped without further fanfare or inconvenience to my client."

"Fine, fine," the officer replied, though they both noticed the disappointment.

"He knew all along you didn't do it," Dave suggested on the way home. "But he was enjoying having you on the witness stand…wanted to make you squirm."

"Yeah, I had him on the witness stand a few years ago…I was young and cocky…I would handle him quite differently now. Forgiveness has never been forthcoming."

"Good lesson for me," Dave observed.

"So what do you make of the messages from Lonnie? Sounds as though he has a private weekend all planned."

Dave was expecting his question. "Yeah, he was pretty adamant that he will not be put off; sounds as though she'll have to pass the weekend before she passes his course."

"So…shouldn't we be doing something about it?"

"Naw. Lee was born a lawyer. She'll handle it; probably wouldn't appreciate my interference. She's smart enough to keep that tape."

"Shouldn't you call her to make sure she does?"

"I'll have to call her to explain my call from the OPP station. How would you like me to explain…?"

"Just tell her the truth."

They sat quietly in the car in the parking lot, needing to talk…yet reluctant.

"Can I ask you something?" Brett began again. Dave nodded. "You don't seem to be at all concerned about this jackal after Lee…yet you were so concerned about *my* relationship with her that you were prepared to leave…?"

Dave looked surprised. "The difference is obvious to me, Brett. Lee can't stand the sight of Lonnie; she's in love with you."

"She told you that?"

"Does she need to tell anybody? My guess is that she'd be heartbroken over your weekending with Rhonda. She'd be crushed."

"And you don't think she went on this weekend to even the score?"

"Not. Definitely not. It's not in her, either to get even, or to disobey her conscience and the Laws of God. Lonnie will soon learn that her convictions mean more to her than passing a course. She will have done her homework; he will have a hard time explaining a failure to the university. She hasn't failed anything in her life. He thinks he can scare her into an affair…obviously doesn't know her!"

"I wish I had your confidence."

"You don't know her either."

"Apparently not. Wish I knew how to get in touch with her."

"Have you tried e-mail?"

"Sent her one every day last week. Told her I was planning to come to Toronto on Monday, and asked her to let me know if she'd be there, and if I could come. She didn't answer. I called, as you heard. She didn't respond. She wasn't there when I got there. Does that sound like she's rather through with me?"

"She may not have read the e-mail. When she's under pressure she ignores stuff like that. She was away when you called…as you know. On the other hand, she may very well decide that she doesn't want…." He paused, noting the blood drain from Brett's face.

"Are you in love with her?"

"You know I am."

"Guess that's why your…why the Rhonda thing threw me for such a loop. Couldn't believe it—choosing Rhonda over Lee!"

Brett contemplated for a few moments. "Guess you…and Lee…don't seem to understand that it was never my intention to trade Lee for Rhonda. In my naivete…stupidity…I didn't think Lee would mind my attending a weekend function with friends…especially since one of them was *her* friend. Initially, I thought she was inviting Lee, too. She muttered something about not having room for any more girls, and I still didn't clue in. Well, anyway, when I told Lee, she was so upset, but she didn't really come apart until I told her who it was. She said she didn't want what was left when Rhonda got through, and left me standing on the step."

"Wow!"

"So what do you suggest?"

Dave sat with his face in his hands for a long moment, then slowly turned to face his friend. "First of all, I think you will have to put the entire relationship into God's hands. Give up your right to…to Lee…."

"That's easy enough for you to say. It seems to me you've had it pretty good with Sherry since you were kids."

"You are right…for the most part. But the Lord brought me to that place of having to give her up a few years ago…hardest thing I've ever done in my entire life. I nearly lost her…to a French maestro…he beguiled her…the wretch!"

"So what did you do?"

"Just what I'm telling you. I had to put her in God's hands and accept what He knew was best. If He allowed her to marry somebody else…. Course I prayed she'd see the light…." He chuckled..

"I can hardly believe that of Sherry. You're so in love."

"We are. We were then, too. It's just that neither of us had dated anyone else. I think she was rather enamoured by his praise of her musical ability…got carried away. Fortunately, she confided in her folks. They sleuthed out a few things. The relationship came to a rather abrupt halt when he invited her to accompany the university orchestra in Montreal. Her dad was rather alarmed…called the hotel and found that he had not arranged for a separate room for her; then he called McGill; they were bringing a pianist in from Paris especially for the concert. The final blow was that he was married. Guess he just wanted a playmate for the weekend. She was pretty crushed. Bob kept me updated, but she was too embarrassed to call. Our moms finally bridged the gap…bless them."

"I'm sorry. I had no idea…."

"Nobody knows…outside the families, I mean. Don't think Lee knows…unless Sherry told her."

"So, even if I give my relationship with Lee over to the Lord…shouldn't I still let her know…?"

"Want to drop her a note on my e-mail? You can be sure she'll read it at least. Does she know you didn't go with Rhonda?"

"If she read my e-mails she does. Otherwise…unless you told her?"

"We don't discuss you, Brett. We decided that when we were both working for you. She was afraid you'd feel ganged up on."

"That's pretty incredible. You two are something else. I'll take you up on the e-mail offer."

"How's the Bible Study comin' along?" Dave asked as they headed into the building.

"Pretty good. I'm learning a lot of things I should have known all along. Finished Genesis…about half way through Exodus. Would be good to have somebody to discuss it with. Are you interested?"

"Yeah. No kidding. How about lunch hours—we could grab a sandwich…."

CHAPTER TWENTY-THREE

"Come in, come in." The dean smiled and motioned her to a chair. "I must say that the materials you dropped off yesterday leave me rather speechless. The situation is much worse than I would have thought. We have had a few complaints over the past two years, but nothing quite as convicting as your tapes, and the statements from your colleagues. Are they willing to discuss this with me?"

"All four of them agreed to do so. Interestingly, each one thought she was the only one."

"That's often the way it is. How are you holding up under the pressure?"

"Amazingly well. Fortunately, I'm too busy to worry about it, and too tired at night to fret."

"What will you do about the weekend he is insisting on?"

"I left a message on his voice mail that the next three weekends are full. That should get me through class time and into exams; I won't have to face him in the classroom anymore. Of course, he'll figure that out and be very indignant."

"Yes, he will…he will indeed." He thought for a few moments, then asked, "Leanne, do you have copies of the class work you have done in this course…anything you've handed in?"

"Yes, I always keep copies of everything."

"Have your marks been good so far?"

"Don't know. Haven't gotten anything from him to date…just reminders that I'm not doing well."

"I'd like to have a copy of everything you've handed in. We'll need to be sure you're treated fairly, though I'd be surprised if he was foolish enough to carry through on his threat."

"I appreciate your concern, Mr. Strauss. I'm really not sure what I would have done…."

"I want to assure you that we are going to deal with this, Leanne. It would be good if we could stall until the semester is over. Please don't feel you need to further endanger yourself on our account. The evidence on hand is sufficient. Feel free to tell him you aren't interested in dating him."

"Thank you for your encouragement, and for the advice. I am looking forward to being done with him…most stressful class I've had in all my years of study."

"Let me know if there's anything I can do…if he becomes too overbearing…."

Thank you, God, she whispered as she made her way to her next class.

❦

"Walker," the voice growled on the other end of the line. "This is Foster—Michael Foster."

"Yes, Michael, what can I do for you?"

"I was in the cafeteria today, UWO; had the unfortunate experience of having my lunch ruined by Lonnie Hencken."

"That's got to be at least an indictable offense."

"That's enough out of you, Walker. Now, I thought I knew Leanne Stevenson pretty well, but what I heard today…."

"Well, she is her own person. Perhaps you would elaborate."

"The rascal had the audacity to expound for the benefit of all within range that Leanne is not only intending to article…but that she's articling with Hencken, Hencken and Mears…" Brett noticed that he spat the name out, before he went on, "and further, he implied there are goings on between them…."

Brett gritted his teeth. "So what do you want from me, Michael?"

"A denial, of course. You know her better than anyone. You were with her when she promised to consider me first. What do you mean, what do I want? I had some sort of a notion that she was your girl…but *Hencken…Lonnie Hencken!*" Again he spat the words.

"It's been a few weeks since we've talked, but I can assure you that she will not be articling with Hencken…wishful thinking on his part. But, tell you what, I'll be in Toronto this afternoon. What if I get back to you on Monday with the official word?"

"Well, I need something official from Leanne…I thought she'd at least be in touch before she made a decision."

"Come now, Foster. She has another whole semester before she has to make up her mind. She makes big decisions slowly and carefully. You'll hear from her."

"I would hope so! *'Lonnie Hencken,'*" he heard him mutter as he hung up.

The rain had turned to sleet by the time he turned off Highway 401 and headed toward the campus of U of T. *The Dean said two o'clock; looks like I'll make it just in time. Sure hope this weather system passes through quickly; it'll be a bearcat trying to get home.*

Her cell phone rang as they finished an afternoon study session and coffee at McDonald's.

"Lee, it's Brett. I'm in town on business. Can I see you?"

"You still know where to find McDonald's?"

"You bet; I'm right near there. Where can I find you?"

"The tables at the back. We've just finished a study session. You can join me for a late coffee."

Her heart jumped as he came into view. It had been more than a month since she'd seen him. *He's more attractive than I remembered,* she mused—*that purposeful masculine stride…his sandy hair windblown…top coat streaked with rain. Looks like a man with a mission.*

She rose quickly and introduced the three students in her study group—Marcelle, Paul and Roberto. Brett greeted them warmly and chatted amiably as they collected notes and loaded backpacks.

"Will you have a coffee?" she asked as he took a seat across from her.

"Guess I do need something. Can we go somewhere…we need to talk, Leanne…I've heard from Foster…." He hoped the *Foster* thing might induce her to consider seeing him.

"I understand there's an ice storm on the way. What could be so important to bring you out in this kind of weather?"

"That's what I need to talk to you about."

She nodded. "I was about to head home to beat the storm. If you want to join me…we could have coffee there. Have you had lunch?"

He shook his head, then suggested. "Okay if I pick up some Chinese food on the way?"

"Fantastic!"

He relieved her of her backpack and computer and followed her to the parking lot. "This weather system means business," he said as he scraped the ice from her windows. "Shall I see you at your place, then?"

What a blessing to have a place like this! she thought to herself as she pulled into her double garage. *Better leave the door open so Brett can park inside. He won't be able to go far tonight…not in these conditions. And if he parks outside, his car will look like an igloo by morning. Wonder if that means I get him for the night?*

She smiled, remembering his little e-mail asking for forgiveness. She had written right back assuring him that she also needed to be forgiven. Her note had been brief, not assuming that they would re-establish the relationship…just assuring him that she carried no ill-will and wishing him well.

She turned up the thermostat. *Another blessing…having a wonderful gas fireplace to take the chill off on nights like this.* She started the coffee, moved her small table near the fireplace and set out plates and flatware. She noted that the windows from the north and west were already heavily coated with ice. *Hope he gets here soon, or he may not make it.*

She heard him pull into the garage and close the automatic door. "Thank you, Lord," she said out loud.

"Pretty wild out there. Looks like I didn't make it to the city any too soon."

"An awful day to come. Maybe we better feed you before you fade away," she suggested as he hung his coat, and she released the delicious aromas in the many small cartons.

"So what brings you out on a day like this?" she asked as she refilled his coffee mug and he stretched his long legs by the fire.

"I want to thank you for seeing me, Lee, and for your hospitality. I'm not presuming that I deserve this time together...but I am grateful."

"I'm glad you've come, Brett. We needed to see each other."

"I had a call from Michael Foster this morning; seems he was having lunch at the cafeteria at UWO, and Lonnie Henchen held forth at length...."

"Oh my!" she interjected. "Whatever was he doing there?"

"Meeting or some such. Anyway, having gained the ear of most of the lawyers and professors present, he proceeded to tell them that you intend to article next year with Hencken, Henchen and Mears, and more...that you and he...." He stopped, not sure just how to proceed.

"Oh, my dear! Brett, is that why you've come out in this weather?"

"Lee, I...I...uh...I needed to see the dean. I'm sorry, I'm sure you'll see it as interference, but he and I discussed Lonnie a few years ago when I was here. I am one of the directors at large of the university, and we discussed certain complaints of several of the female students at that time.

"I must say 'thank you' for allowing us to access your answering machine a few weeks ago; but as you know...for me, at least...it was a mixed blessing. When I heard Lonnie trying to exploit you...trying to force you into a weekend with him.... Well, I was ready to come right then, but Dave said you'd handle it...that you'd resent being rescued...that you were born a lawyer...that you'd look after yourself. It's been pretty hard to wait...and wonder.

"Today when Foster called and I found out that Lonnie was spouting this stuff, I knew I had to see the dean."

"So you know what's been going on?"

"I do now. Strauss was some surprised that I didn't know…that you hadn't even asked Dave for advice. Sounds like you've handled things pretty well."

"I didn't know who to trust at first. Didn't know whether contacting Dean Strauss was the way to go…thought he might think I was just a student who didn't like homework…wanting to get even with her prof. I didn't have liberty to contact you, Brett…though I thought of it a dozen times, and wanted to."

"I wish you had." His face showed deep emotion.

"I don't know what to do now. I am feeling harassed…he's determined to pull this weekend thing off before the end of classes. I think he's gone beyond the rational…calls me repeatedly…leaves silly messages. The dean says to just say 'no, I'm not going.' But I still have two weeks of class, and I haven't really told Mr. Strauss…." She paused as if she really shouldn't say anything further.

"Tell me, Lee."

"Well, I've taken to looking over my shoulder this last couple of weeks. He seems to be following me; I just get my computer set up in the library, and he's there. If I stop for a burger at McD's or a soup at Tim's, he shows up. I'm wondering if he's losing it. I'm not sure how to handle the situation. I have a lot of heavy class work to finish…I need the time to concentrate, prep for finals. It's getting to be quite unnerving. Maybe *stalked* is too strong a word…."

"Sounds to me like you're using the right word. You need to report this to the police."

"I'm not sure I have enough evidence."

"Did you save the tape, the one we listened to?"

"Yes. I gave a copy of it to the dean. Also I recorded a couple of conversations I had with Lonnie, and gave them to him."

"Do you have copies of all of those?"

She nodded.

"Would you mind playing them for me?"

"Not at all, but the one in the restaurant is over two hours, and I have copies of all the phone messages. Are you sure…?"

"Absolutely. Why don't we listen to the shorter ones first, and if you don't mind, I can listen to the longer one when I get to my hotel."

"Hotel?" she asked with surprise. "Are you really planning to go back out in this? I don't think we can get the garage door open. Are you frightened to stay here? I do have two guest rooms, you know."

He contemplated for a few seconds. "Lee, I don't want to compromise your reputation. I did call after we left McD's and reserved a room."

"Who do you think might be out in this storm, checking out my company?" She laughed.

"Unless it's Lonnie." He smirked. "Well, if you're sure…I would enjoy spending the evening with you…."

He started as his cell phone rang, and retrieved it from his briefcase. "Well, hello there, Dave. I'm very fine, thank you…indeed I did…got here just before the real stuff started. No, I won't even try to drive tonight. Ice on the doorsill is already a few inches thick. Hope the electrical holds up." He paused, then answered, "Actually, I'm at Lee's. Looks like I'm here for the night. Hope that doesn't rattle you too much…. Sure I will, if she lets me…and thanks for your concern. I'll keep in touch," he said as he signed off.

So Dave had sent her a hug! She was glad Brett was exercising discretion.

She watched his face as they listened to the tapes. His jaw muscles clenched from time to time, and his colour heightened. He was clearly outraged. She hadn't listened to them since they were recorded…somehow it had seemed like replaying a nightmare. She had missed a lot of the things he said…now she realized just how forceful he had been. Closing her eyes, she thanked God for the emotional stamina and wisdom He had given her.

"Lee, you need to take these to the police and tell them what you suspect…about his following you."

"What will be gained from that?"

"If he continues…and it seems he is determined to have you one way or another…you can call and they'll have something to go on…know that it's serious."

"Wouldn't I just be pulling the rug on the dean? And with this ice storm, the police will be overwhelmed…."

"Wait until the aftermath of the storm is over. As for the dean…frankly, I'm surprised…indignant…make that outraged…that he knows all this, and Lonnie is still on the loose…and you and countless others are still at risk. I have a mind…!"

"Hold it, right there!"

"Sorry. Is that interference?"

"I know you're concerned."

"Why can't you accept help, Lee? Why so independent?"

"Maybe I just haven't found anyone I can depend on?"

"OUCH! OUCH! Guess I have that coming."

"That wasn't really aimed at you. Just the story of my life. You know it's nearly 11:00; time we got horizontal. Looks like we may have more time to visit tomorrow," she said, looking at the ice-coated windows. "I'd like to hear about the young offenders. I know they got suspended sentences…saw that in *The Star*, but I'd like to hear how things went there…and Tony—what's happening with him."

He nodded, smiled. "Thanks again, Lee. See you in the morning."

CHAPTER TWENTY-FOUR

He slept fitfully. Each time he woke he was drenched in sweat...the blankets and sheets askew. The dream! He had all but trashed the lovely bed. He hoped he hadn't disturbed Lee...that she hadn't heard the thrashing. *Oh, God, I've got to do something about this*, he moaned.

Rain still beating on the windows. Looks like I'll be here for a while; hope Leanne doesn't get antsy having me around for so long. He lay for a few moments smelling the coffee, then, *Please, God, help us to have the kind of talk that will clear the air between us. You know the situation so much better than either of us. Thank you for bringing me safely yesterday, and for the time I've already had here.*

She heard his shower and started the ham omelette.

"Temperature has gone up," she offered as he came through the door a few minutes later. It's raining. Look at the window in the family room—ice is already thinning. By noon we should be prisoners no more."

He received the news with mixed emotions. Good to know the storm had passed, sorry that his time with Lee would be cut short. He would have to choose his topics carefully.

"I take it you didn't sleep well," she offered hesitantly. "Bed not to your liking?"

"Actually...I...uh...." He hesitated, slightly embarrassed. "Why do you think that?"

"I heard you cry out...you seemed to be thrashing about...." She looked at him questioningly.

"Yeah, guess I was at that. I'm sorry I disturbed you. I've been having nightmares...."

"An ongoing thing?"

"Mostly just when I'm under stress...." He stopped, realizing he had revealed more than he intended.

"You would seem to be in the wrong profession to avoid stress."

"It's not the profession that gives me stress...it seems to be...." Again he stopped.

"So?"

"I guess I would have to say it's more emotional stuff. I would really not like to get into it right now, if you don't mind."

"Sorry, I didn't mean to pry. More coffee?" She held up the carafe.

<hr />

"That was one mighty fine breakfast," he commented as they carried their coffee into the family room. "Do you like to read the Scriptures in the morning?"

"Yes, I do. Usually I take time with the Lord before breakfast, but I'd enjoy having you read, if you'd like."

He opened his briefcase and removed his new Bible. "I read this Psalm the other day and found it really spoke to me. Okay if I share it?"

"By all means."

He began slowly reading Psalm 51 in the New International Version:

Have mercy on me, O God, according to your unfailing love;
according to your great compassion, blot out my transgressions.
Wash away all my iniquity and cleanse me from my sin.
For I know my transgressions, and my sin is always before me.
Against you, you only, have I sinned and done what is evil in your sight,....
Create in me a pure heart, O God, and renew a steadfast spirit within me....
Restore to me the joy of your salvation and grant me a willing spirit, to
sustain me...

The sacrifices of God are a broken spirit; a broken and contrite heart,
O God, you will not despise.

(Psalm 51:1-4,10,12,17 NIV)

"What do you find so moving about it, Brett?" she asked as he finished and sat silently for a few seconds.

"It's what David prayed after he had committed adultery with Bathsheba, and had her husband murdered. God sent the prophet Nathan…."

"Yes, I'm familiar." She waited.

"I…I haven't done what David did, Lee, but the weight of sin is the same…I sinned against God…and you…when I betrayed the trust you had in me. I want you to know, though, that I didn't go out with Rhonda…not for the weekend, not any time. She was outraged…threatened me…that's why she charged me with assault. Course I wasn't there…I was in Toronto waiting for you to come home."

"I didn't know…I didn't know what your plans…."

"I gather you didn't read my e-mails."

She shook her head. "I couldn't bear to hear from you, Brett. I just hit the delete button whenever your name appeared on my screen. I didn't need to hear how you and Rhonda…."

"I can't tell you how sorry I am for my foolishness. When Dave told me who she was and how she operates, I couldn't look at myself in the mirror. Couldn't believe I had even allowed her to have coffee with me…even though she invited herself."

She sat quietly without comment.

"Tell me what happened the night I told you about Rhonda. I didn't think I had said anything to injure you…I really thought you wouldn't mind my doing a favour for an old friend of yours."

"Well, I guess you must know now that she was never my friend. She hasn't that capacity. But the night in question…do we really have to go through all this?"

"Please."

"Brett, the day we spent together was one of the most enjoyable experiences of my life. We laughed, played, ate together, and just enjoyed each other. It had been a perfect day. When we arrived at my door…I wasn't sure whether you intended to come in for a while since it was only around seven. When you turned to me and said there was something you needed to tell me…I…I," she faltered; a slight blush creeping up her neck. "I really wasn't expecting you to say, 'I've been seeing someone else.'"

"Lee, I am so sorry. I can hardly believe how clumsy…stupid…it wasn't what I intended to say at all. I made it sound like I was dating somebody else."

"Yes. You did. And when I found out who it was…my world fell apart. I don't know if I have ever experienced that much emotional pain…except when my folks died. I felt betrayed. Guess I kept wondering why you didn't tell me this at the beginning of the day…why you came to Toronto and spent the day with me—you toyed with me—and all the while you knew you planned to spend the weekend with Rhonda. I cried…for a very long time…then spent some time with the Lord…prayed he'd keep you…give you wisdom. Gave up any claim that I thought I had to your affections…."

"Lee…Lee." He wanted desperately to take her in his arms, and knew he no longer had the right. "I know that God has forgiven me for my duplicity. Will you?"

"I think I have, Brett. I'm not sure what forgiveness looks like to you. I'm not holding any grudges…don't wish you any harm…pray for your happiness…hope we can be friends."

His eyes were sad as they looked into hers. "Do you think you might ever come to the place…guess I thought that we…did you ever love me…ever dream that…?"

"Yes, I did…I did dream. When I came back from England…guess I went there to sort out my feelings for you…."

"And now…you've put them on the shelf?"

"No. No shelf. I think I let them die that night; I heard once that when dreams die, you need to dream new ones. I haven't had time for that yet; I'm operating on numb right now."

"Did you love me, Lee?"

"It's irrelevant, Brett. Guess what happened has made me realize how little I know about you. Don't really know who you are. Too many unanswered questions."

"Will you let me answer them for you?"

"Is that important to you…that I know who you are?"

He nodded. "Very."

"Can I ask why?"

"A number of reasons. Dave and I are talking partnership as soon as he finishes his articles. I keep hoping…maybe praying is more honest…that you'll join us one day. More than that, Lee…I'm hoping…praying…that one day…." He stopped, dropping his hands with a helpless gesture…realizing the timing was bad. "You must know I love you, Lee…since that first day you walked into my office and told me, 'You are done, Mr. Walker…quite done!'"

She smiled. "Awfully crass of me."

"I love you, Lee," he repeated. "I love you. I should have told you that day in the park…guess I wanted it to be a special occasion…I sure blew that one."

She did not respond.

"Lee," his voice was almost pleading. "I need to know if you want me out of your life. If you do, you need to say so and…and…I won't…."

The surprise showed on her face. "That's not fair!" she managed. "You know I haven't had time to sort out my feelings with everything else going on…I value your friendship. Why do you need to know this right now? You aren't playing fair…."

"I'm sorry. I didn't mean to put you on the spot…give you more stress. Guess I need to know if you care…at all…."

"Of course I care. I'm not sure about…a relationship, but I'm glad you didn't weekend with Rhonda. She would have ruined you. I doubt she'll give up so easily…she'll be outraged. I do want us to be good friends. I haven't the capacity to look any farther ahead than that. I'll write Mr. Foster at once…he'll just have to be patient with me."

"Guess I'd better get myself together and get out of your way," he commented as he stood up. "Lee, will you promise me that you'll call if I can help in any way with the Hencken thing?"

"Why would I do that?"

"Because I'm on the board—it's my business, too. But more than that, we're friends, Lee, and you may need a good lawyer; and...and because I love you."

"Thank you, Brett. I'll take all that into account should the need arise."

"Can I deliver the hug?" he asked as he took his farewell.

She smiled and moved into his arms. He held her as long as he dared.

The familiar feeling of security in his arms...his closeness...the smell of his aftershave overwhelmed her. She stiffened indignantly and backed away. "That didn't feel like a Dave hug."

"Perhaps with a little practice," he countered.

"Goodbye, Brett."

"Hope to see you soon," he whispered. "Keep in touch."

Goodbye, Brett. It echoed in his mind as he turned onto the 401. It sounded too final!

CHAPTER TWENTY-FIVE

Dear Mr. Foster. She wrote quickly as though she wanted to get him off her mind. *Thank you for your enquiry via Mr. Brett Walker. My semester has been long and heavy, leaving little time for contemplation of my future. I do intend, however, to have an answer for you early in the New Year, and I will be in touch immediately once that decision is made. Thank you again for considering me. I appreciate your interest. Leanne Stevenson.*

She paused briefly, then added: *Copy to Brett Walker.*

She clicked over to *Send and Receive*, noting she had mail. A note from Dave and Sherry wanting to come next weekend. Sherry had Monday off.

She did a quick reply. *Love to have you come Friday to Sunday, but I'll be in class Monday.*

She let the phone ring. As she suspected, another call from Lonnie. He had called every day—pleading, warning, threatening, entreating. *He's right off his rocker; he needs help*, she decided as she went back to her studies.

She dreaded his classes. *Only two more weeks to go—four classes with Hencken—I'll make it. I'll be free of him. Let the dean's office do what they will after that!*

It would be so good to see Dave and Sherry. She'd missed Sherry's good fun…Dave's sage advice—even if she didn't take it most of the time. Good to run some of this Hencken and Foster stuff by Dave. She'd enjoy his insights.

"Little sis, it's time for a talk with big brother." He smiled as he pushed back his chair and stretched his legs under the small table.

"Why don't you two sit by the fire, and let me tidy up here?" Sherry suggested.

How like her, Lee thought as they took her up on her offer.

"Tell me," she started, "what is going on with the three young offenders. I understand they got suspended sentences?"

"Yeah. They were first-time offenders. Their crime really occasioned by Tony Cortez; the Court rightly observed that they probably never would have come up with the idea on their own…particularly Rob Chambers. A really nice kid! His dad asked for counseling and Brett put them in touch with Reverend Bill Somerville. He really does know his stuff around teens and families. Seems the Chambers were church folk years ago…just drifted away. Needless to say, that has been rectified. Guess Bert's whole attitude changed when he realized his son had tried to protect him by co-operating with what he considered a biker gang. He came up to the office to thank Brett…a very tearful reunion with his son, apparently."

"And the other two?"

"Jerry Coombs will do okay, I think. His dad is an old friend of Brett. They seem to do a reasonable job of parenting. The Dewalt boy, Janet's son, Dan…don't know what will happen to that poor kid. She's not much of a role model. Pastor tried to get him into the youth group…give him a different point of reference. She didn't encourage it at all. Tried her jolly best to get Brett's attention."

"So how is Gregg Romero doing? He must have been pretty traumatized after finding the guard…then being charged."

"No kidding. He's been in counseling ever since. A lot of nightmares. Seems to be coming along pretty good, from what I hear."

"And what's happening with Tony Cortez?"

"Some good things, I think. But I'd rather that Brett told you about that situation. He's pretty involved there."

"He didn't comment on it when he was here…course he was pretty emotionally involved in the Hencken thing."

"Tell me about that, Lee. Help me to understand what's going on there. I hear rumours that you may article with Hencken."

"That's all they are—rumours. Were you really going to article with him before Brett's offer?"

"Course not. My offer was from Mears. Not that I would have minded the elder Hencken being my advisor, but Lonnie…not a chance!"

"Glad you clarified that little point, big brother. You might have led me astray," she said with a grin. "Anyway, as to Lonnie…I think he's slipped a few cogs. Guess he's always intimidated students into weekends with him in exchange—supposedly—for marks. He's been after me all semester. I'm not sure why he's picked on me."

"Beauty and intelligence are always attractive."

"The university is full of beautiful, intelligent gals. His class is not lacking…."

"So why do you think he's after you?"

"Maybe because I've outwitted him so far…sees me as a personal challenge. He's gotten really strange…calls my answering machine pretty much every day…resorts to threats and whining. I think he's really lost it. Become obsessive. I've two more classes with him…can't wait to be done. He keeps issuing veiled threats that I'm not understanding the class work…that I will need to pass his course to graduate."

"So how are you responding. Have you reported any of this to anyone?"

"Oh, sure. I've recorded some of our conversations and given them to the dean, along with those from my answering machine. He hopes to pull the plug as soon as the semester is over. Lonnie is apparently seeking tenure; they want him out of there."

"How do you respond to being used in that way? What's in this for you if you put up with this incredible stress till the end of the semester, then he get's fired? You'll need some protection from him. He's needs to be brought to the attention of the police. At the very least, you should have a restraining order."

She sat silently, contemplating what her brother had just said, moreso because it echoed her own thoughts. "Brett would like it if I let him handle it for me; I'm not sure I want him involved."

"Maybe we need to talk about that, Lee. And about your future. I take it that you are considering private practice...that you do intend to article."

"I'm leaning pretty heavy that way."

"Would you really consider articling with Foster...vis-a-vis Brett Walker?"

"I intend to wade my way through that over the holidays, but yes, I am seriously considering."

"Why?"

"Several reasons. For one, Brett has never asked me to article with him. In some ways, I feel like I've already articled with him. Secondly, working with the two of you...."

"Go on."

"I doubt that I would ever be taken seriously as a lawyer. I'm Brett's *Girl Friday* and your little sis. Not much to build a career on."

"Wow! Sorry! Guess I never really gave that aspect of it much thought. You must know, though, how much Brett admires your insight and expertise. I do, too, sis. The way you took over Dad's practice this last year...you were pretty well articled before you went back to school."

"Guess I feel like that. It's a bit exasperating for me...sitting in a classroom of students who know so little of what life is really like in the legal world...then having Lonnie expound on stuff I know he's never tried in his life. I'll be glad to be done."

"So why would you go with Foster?"

"A good offer. It won't be as good as it looks of course, but maybe I can learn a few things in the area of estates; I think that's probably my area of interest."

"You know why Foster wants you, don't you?"

"Because I'm such a good lawyer!" she smirked.

"And because you're such a good lawyer, there are a few dozen of Dad's clients waiting for you to settle down so they can come. In these last few weeks we've had three calls, asking if the Stevenson working with Mr. Walker was Leanne Stevenson. Two of them finally condescended to see me, on the promise that you would soon be back in the area. Don't think for a moment that Foster doesn't know that you'll bring a following with you…and that they just might stay…even if you leave. He's very shrewd…an eye for business."

"I've thought of that. Didn't realize that there would be more than a few. I really would like to see you and Brett benefit from Dad's clients."

"Maybe if you and Brett could resolve your differences…?"

"I was actually considering Foster when I was still going with Brett."

"That sounds terribly past tense."

She nodded.

"Didn't he spend the weekend with you?"

"Course. He got iced in."

"Sounds like he was *iced* in more ways than one."

She made a face.

"Really, Lee, I think this whole thing is tied together. You'd enjoy working with Brett; you did before. You know him well enough to know that he would give you whatever you want to make you happy. He's saving that gorgeous office next to his for someone special. It would sure have been handy for me—connecting doors and all—but he never offered it to me. He sent me off across the hall."

"You're hardly abused—ceiling-to-floor windows, oak trim, shelving, all the etceteras."

"Who's complaining? Just making an observation. I know jolly well he's keeping it for you…and you know it, too."

"Maybe we could just leave my personal life out of this."

"Don't think so, Lee. You'll need to settle with Brett before you can move on. I know you're in love with him—hurt and angry, yes, but in love nevertheless."

"That's enough now, Dave. You leave her alone."

He looked up, surprised that Sherry had spoken up. He was used to her accepting his decisions.

"That's enough *big brothering* for one weekend. Why don't we go for a nice long walk?"

The phone rang and Dave paused to listen as Lonnie read the riot act to Lee. He was coming to her house on Tuesday at seven. She had better be there…time was running out.

"Good heavens, Lee. You put up with that. You need to call the police."

"Actually, he's picked a good evening. My study group meets here from seven until around eleven."

"Leanne, you need to call the police."

"Leave her alone, Dave. She's smart enough to know what to do."

"You know I just want to protect her, sweetheart."

"Yeah, it's okay, Sherry," Lee commented as they started on their walk. "I know Dave loves me; he has my best interests at heart. He just tends to overdo a little on the direction and the protection from time to time."

In spite of being glad to see her brother and sister-in-law, she was relieved when Sunday afternoon rolled around. Lonnie had left two more calls, and Dave was visibly anxious for her well-being.

"Promise me you'll call if you need help," he insisted.

"Brett has already offered. How much help can one student handle?" she joked.

In spite of her bravado and the need for solitude, she felt a sudden pang of fear and aloneness as she watched the Honda disappear around the crescent. How would she really handle Lonnie if he persisted? She could call Brett but he was at least two hours away. The dean? He hadn't really helped so far. She would take Dave's advice and call the police. Yes, if he became obnoxious, she would take steps to protect herself.

Having made that decision, she set about preparing herself for her two Monday classes…another one with Hencken would be over with…then one more on Thursday. If she could just hang on….

In spite of her positive self-talk, she found herself looking over her shoulder as she arrived home from Sunday evening worship. She closed the garage door quickly behind her and entered the house through the adjoining one. The feeling persisted. She started in the basement and checked room by room. Nothing. *Get a grip, Leanne; you're starting to lose it*, she warned herself.

She slept fitfully. Suddenly Lonnie was standing in her bedroom, looking at her...the window open...curtains blowing in the wind. Her screams shook her out of the nightmare, but her rest was over. How would she cope if this continued?

CHAPTER TWENTY-SIX

She decided to skip Lonnie's class Monday morning. She could get notes from Marcia. If she stayed home and worked on her final assignment, and maybe caught a quick nap, she would be awake and alert for her afternoon class. With a little luck, and a good sleep tonight, she might be able to get through Tuesday.

The phone rang as she prepared her supper. She let the answering machine take over and found herself shuddering as she listened, "So...you decided to skip my class this morning! You know what happens to girls who do that, don't you? Just remember we have a date tomorrow night...at your place...at seven."

Too bad for you, Lonnie, she mused. *My study group will be here from seven till 11:00.* She couldn't force herself to think what might happen after 11:00. Surely, he would have given up by then. *Oh, God, I'll need some direction...some protection here.*

Her sleep was less than she had hoped for. *Thank you, Lord, no nightmare,* she whispered in her morning prayers. *Please help me through the day...give me some assurance that I'm protected...that You're watching over me.*

She studied till 10:00, then prepared for an 11:00 o'clock class. She glanced at the call display as her phone rang...surely not Lonnie *again*...this early in the day. *No, not Lonnie.* She picked it up quickly and recognized Brett's voice.

"Hello, Lee, I'm in town. Can you meet me for lunch?"

"Yes," she said with an overwhelming sense of relief. She hung up without even asking what he was doing in town this early on Tuesday morning.

"Are you wondering what I'm doing in town today?" he asked as they waited for their lunch.

"Are you here on account of me?"

He declined to answer directly. "Well, Dave did tell me about your *date* with Lonnie tonight, and I wondered how you would cope with that. I do have some research I can do at the library, and I…I…if you don't mind my hanging around…."

She put her hands over her face and let the tears come. "You're the answer to my prayer," she explained through her sobs. "I asked God this morning to give me some assurance that I was protected…that He was watching over me…and He sent you."

"Thank you, Lee." He reached across the table and squeezed her hand. "Thank you for sharing that with me. I really did feel an urgency about this, and the more I prayed, the more urgent it became. Dave was pretty exercised about the whole thing."

"Thank you for coming, Brett. You can't imagine my relief; Lonnie has been right off the wall. I'm not sure what he'll do tonight when he finds my study group at my house from seven till eleven."

"I plan to be there, Lee. Get my car into your garage ahead of time so he doesn't know I'm there. I won't disturb your studies; I can…."

"Would you like to give us some pointers? I'm sure the group would love it."

"If that works for everybody, I'd be glad to. Maybe I can pick up some chicken and ribs for supper and we'll eat at your house. In fact, if you give me a key, I could be there by 5:00. It should be early enough to avoid surveillance."

"You certainly think of everything," she said as she handed over the key.

Her heart was light as she headed home at 5:30. *Thank you, God,* she whispered again and again. How different she felt about this evening. The group would just love having Brett there, she told herself. *Admit it,*

Lee, you're going to love having Brett there. And the threat of Lonnie had all but disappeared. Brett would know what to do.

She smelled supper as she removed her coat and boots. "Wow, I don't often have maid service," she complimented, then noticed the vase of roses in the center of the table.

She stood motionless, not quite sure how to respond to his obvious devotion.

"I thought…you might need a little encouragement," he suggested hopefully.

"Thank you, Brett. You *are* thoughtful, but your being here is encouragement enough."

He reviewed the calls she had saved from the past week. "He really is getting more persistent and more ridiculous all the time. If he tries anything unreasonable tonight, Lee…you know…he must be dealt with." He spoke hesitantly, expecting resistance from her.

"I know. I've already decided that I'll need to call the police. If I leave it for the dean, I think he'll be satisfied with a resignation. That leaves Lonnie free to simply teach somewhere else and start all over again…and it leaves me no protection from him. More than that, I'm seeing that he can be quite vicious. No telling what he'll try when he knows I started all this…taped his conversations…saved his phone calls…reported to the dean. I'll be a sitting duck."

He looked surprised. "What brought you to that conclusion?"

"You and Dave. I really do listen, you know. Just don't like having my decisions made for me."

He smiled. "I figured that out all by myself."

"And besides," she went on, "he's getting really silly. I think he may need some psychiatric help. He seems to be obsessed with…."

He nodded.

"This is simply scrumptious," she said, licking her fingers. "A really neat idea. Thank you, Brett, for coming, and being here with me."

"Pleasure's all mine. Need some help?" he asked, taking her hand and licking the sauce off her fingers.

This is too much like old times, and it's a little scary, she thought as she enjoyed the easy comradery.

Her study group responded enthusiastically to Brett's insights. *Too bad he doesn't instruct this class*, Lee found herself thinking more than once. She saw a whole new side of him—fun…creativity. He was obviously enjoying himself. This must have been the Brett that Dave knew from the classroom. No wonder he accepted the offer to article with him so quickly! *This is a Brett that I don't know anything about*, she mused.

No word from Lonnie. He must have come by and noticed the cars. She wondered if he would just bide his time…waiting for her to be alone.

Brett waited in the family room while she bade goodnight to her fellow students. "No point in my appearing at the door," he suggested. "If he wants to close in on you, better he should do so tonight. I certainly won't be comfortable going home with him on the loose."

"This is terribly frightening," she said as she joined him by the fire. "Whatever would I do if I were alone? I'm nearly hysterical as it is."

"No need. He may not even come tonight…." He broke off as the doorbell rang.

"What shall I do?" she whispered.

"Why not ask who's there. Don't open the door."

"Hello, who's there?"

"Leanne! How dare you do this to me! Treat me like this! Open this door at once!"

"I'm sorry I can't do that, Lonnie. You need to go home and get a good rest. It's nearly 11:30 and I have a very busy day tomorrow."

"Busy indeed! You were too busy to bother showing up for my class. OPEN THIS DOOR AT ONCE!" he yelled as he pounded his fists on the door.

Brett motioned for her to join him in the family room. "Let's wait. If he tries to break in, you need to call 9-1-1. Better they should catch him in the act of something illegal, so they'll at least hold him for the night."

They waited as he ranted and raved. They heard him open his car door, then close it forcefully. "Maybe he's leaving," she whispered.

She was glad for the adjoining condos; at least he couldn't get through to the back…all those big windows…a scary thought!

Suddenly the front door shuddered as he attacked it with a blunt instrument.

"He won't get through that door...unless he gets an axe. He'd be smarter to try a window," Brett smirked.

"He doesn't need any suggestions from you."

As if he overheard their conversation, the noise shifted to the small front window. She heard him throw off the screen and begin to pry.

"It's time to call, Lee."

She dialed quickly. "It's Leanne Stevenson," she said breathlessly, then quickly gave her address. "Someone is trying to break into my house."

"Help is on the way; we've just had a call from your neighbour."

As he spoke several police cars converged in front of the house. Lonnie's screams and obscenities were proof that he had been caught red-handed.

Brett came behind her as she answered the doorbell.

"Do you know this assailant?"

"Yes, yes, I do. He's one of my professors; I'm a law student. He's actually been harassing me all semester."

"Would you be willing to accompany me to the police station and give us a statement?"

"Yes, we would, officer," Brett answered for her.

"And you are?"

"Brett Walker, Solicitor. I'm acting on behalf of Miss Stevenson. Mr. Hencken has been threatening her for some time. She would like to press charges." He looked at Leanne for her approval.

She nodded.

"We'll follow you," he suggested to the officer. "Lee, you'll need to take along those tapes. Do you have copies?"

She nodded as she hurried to comply, and slipped the last tape from her answering machine. "Guess I don't have a copy of this one—the one where he threatened to come after me tonight."

"Then let's make a quick copy. Don't want that one to get lost."

"Officer, why don't you step inside for a minute?" she invited. "We need to make a copy of this tape before we turn it over. It's rather cool out there."

She heard the other two cars pull away and assumed that Lonnie had been escorted off her premises. She hoped her nightmare was over…and not just beginning.

The next two hours were a blur as she answered questions, gave a statement, and presented her evidence. "I can't prove it," she admitted, "but this last while I'm sure he's been stalking me. He shows up when I'm studying, waiting for a friend, having lunch…it just goes on and on. He seems to be everywhere. Guess I think he needs some help…."

"We will look this over, ma'am, and charge him accordingly. He certainly was determined to gain forcible entry, and his behaviour…."

"It's nearly 2:30," she said as they headed home. "Glad I don't have any classes today."

"Okay if I spend what's left of the night? I'd like to see Dean Strauss tomorrow before I head back."

"I'd actually be more comfortable if you'd stay. I'm still feeling antsy about all this."

"Do you have more classes?"

"No. Guess I won't have one with Lonnie on Thursday…boy I hope not. Do you think he'll be out of there and back in the classroom?"

"He may be out, but he won't be back in the classroom. Not ever, if I can help it! Lee, you need to go after him for all the distress he's caused you. And what about the four gals that gave statements to the dean? Didn't you say Lonnie actually succeeded…?"

"Yes, apparently. If they think there's a chance, my guess is they'll want to nail him."

"Will you come back to London with me this afternoon? You need to distance yourself from this thing…get a new perspective before you get into finals. Don't you have next week off—reading week? You're pretty stressed, it seems to me."

"I don't know. If I come I should bring my own car so I'll have a way back."

"I'd like to take you home, Lee…and bring you back. I think you'd relax a lot more if someone else was driving. You're pretty uptight."

"Lets talk about it after we've had some sleep. My mind is way too fuzzy to make such a major decision." She smiled.

CHAPTER TWENTY-SEVEN

UNIVERSITY PROFESSOR ARRESTED: Breaking and Entering...Sexual Harassment Charges. The headline shouted from the morning paper, as they faced off with a pale and angry Dean Strauss.

"What do you mean by pulling a stunt like this?" he addressed his question to Leanne.

"I'm representing Leanne; you might address your questions to me. What does she mean? She means to stop the harassment...the threats...the attempted unlawful entry of last evening. Something you have failed to do in all these months, I might add."

"I am certainly disappointed...disappointed that you have cast the university in such a bad light. If you could have held on till the end of the semester...surely that's not too much to ask...we would have dealt with him...he would have been dismissed. This whole thing could have been handled much more discreetly...."

"You're disappointed, Dean Strauss? From the recordings that Leanne left with you, and the statements of four of your students, you know what this man is doing. What steps have you taken to protect these girls? The police apprehended this man, Lonnie, trying to gain entry into Leanne's house, all the while uttering threats. Should she just have allowed this, so you could save face?"

The dean's face turned from white to red as he tried to regain his composure.

"Fortunately, he left his threat on her answering machine, which is why I came from London to protect her. Good thing I did. At the very least you owe these students an apology…at the most—you may well have a lawsuit on your hands."

"You have made a laughing stock of the university…this whole thing could have been handled discreetly…."

"You mean it could have been covered up," Brett countered, "leaving Hencken free to manipulate students in another university. The public has a right to be protected. You've known for years he's a predator. It's time he was exposed…his preying days over."

The dean's face was back to white, his lips set in a thin line. "Of course he will not be teaching here any longer…you have seen to that." He turned to Leanne.

"Thank you." She tried a smile. "I'm happy to accept responsibility."

⟨⟩

"I need to go home and pick up some things before I go," she commented as they left the campus, "and I think I should call those four gals and ask them if they'd like to go to the police station and give statements."

"Good idea. Do you think they might?"

"Three of them will, the fourth…maybe."

"Tell me something," he ventured as they joined in the flow of late-afternoon traffic.

"What would you like to know?"

"Well, I guess…I find myself wondering from time to time…who is *Bill?* And is he the reason you could just drop me off your roster so quickly?" He chanced a look at her.

"How do you know about Bill?"

"You mentioned him in your talk with Lonnie…in the restaurant; you were picking him up at the airport at 10:30."

"You don't miss much, I must say. Yes, there is a Bill…he's a good friend. I met him in church the first Sunday evening I was in Toronto; he was on the welcoming committee."

"So?"

"So what?"

"So what does he do? What does he mean to you? Is he that new dream you just haven't had time for? Does he know about the stress you've had with Lonnie?"

"Wow! One thing at a time! Bill is an interior designer. I consider him a good friend. I offered to drop him at the airport and pick him up when his car was in the garage for repairs. We don't know each other well, but commiserated when we each suffered a break-down in a special relationship. Bill's lady friend wanted to move in with him; he wanted to marry. She refused and moved in with someone else; he was devastated. He doesn't know much about Lonnie; he's been in New York for the last couple of weeks...trade show or whatever."

"So?"

"So what?"

"Is he the new dream you're working on?"

"Honestly, Brett, you must think I'm superwoman. The only dream I'm working on is to find my way out of this nightmare."

"So, does Bill know about me?"

"Of course."

"What does he know about me?"

"Knows you are a lawyer...that I worked for you...that I was very fond of you...that I thought you were fond of me...that you found someone else...that I was devastated. Guess that about covers it."

They lapsed into silence for some miles as he tried to think of a way to overcome the barrier his questioning had obviously created. Thankfully, the music from the CD seemed to make the silence less threatening.

"I'm sorry, Lee," he began, "sorry I seem to ask all the wrong questions. I hope you know how precious you are to me." He glanced over, then took her hand and held it.

She let her hand remain in his; it felt warm and secure. "I know you care for me, Brett, and under all the numbness and stress that I'm feeling right now, I know that I also care for you. I know myself well enough to know that I can't turn my feelings off like a water tap."

"I called Dave. He knows you're with me. Actually, he asked me to bring you home, if you'd consider coming. But I would really like to stop and have supper somewhere, so we can have a little time together that's…hopefully…stress free. Can you go with that?"

She nodded.

He lost no time in finding a restaurant with a quiet, secluded table. Soft music, lovely atmosphere. *Almost like a date*, she decided.

"Dave tells me that I have neglected to invite you to article with us?"

"You and Dave seem to be discussing me rather freely these days. What else does he tell you?"

"That you're afraid to come on board with us…afraid you won't be taken seriously as a partner."

"Anything else I should know about?"

"Yes, Lee, there are some things. First of all, I know I can't compete with Foster…either in experience, opportunity or salary. I know it would be a good opportunity—one I can't provide. Even if he wants to take advantage of your father's clients, you would still benefit. Foster is a good lawyer—astute, honest, good head for business. Besides all that, he obviously knows you and has a great deal of respect for you. He had the audacity to offer Dave a position as soon as he's through articling. He doesn't miss a trick."

"I thought Dave was going into partnership with you."

"Yes, he has decided to come on board…thank the Lord. Guess I thought you knew how much I want you to work with us…in whatever capacity you choose. Would love to have you article…and, no, you wouldn't be my *Girl Friday*. If you remember, we have a secretary, trained…in part at least…by an expert."

She made a face, as he continued. "I've told you before that I would love to have you work with me. I would do my best for you…give you opportunities in your areas of interest. I would take you on the same pay scale where I started Dave. Will you come to the office and go over it with me while you're here?"

"You are quite a guy!"

"Is that a 'yes'?"

"How could it be anything else with an offer like that?"

"Shall we say tomorrow morning then? How's 11:00? Maybe we could have lunch somewhere."

"Sounds fine. It'll give me a little time to sleep in; feel like I've been short-changed these last few weeks. Last night was almost not there."

"You do look awfully weary, Lee. Are you feeling okay?"

"Probably nothing that a few good nights of sleep won't fix. Thanks for bringing me home; I really needed to get away from the rat race."

Thank you, Lord, thank you, he whispered. "Let me help you with that," he said as she picked up her jacket. "You've just made my day." He smiled as he slipped an arm around her and guided her from the restaurant.

Chapter Twenty-Eight

He looked up as Dave paused briefly in the doorway of this office. "Mornin', Brett."

"Morning, Dave. You look like a man with something on his mind."

"Just took Lee to the hospital. She was blacking out...doc took one look and put her in."

"Does he know...?"

"Not yet. Took a bunch of blood tests...put her on intravenous. Apparently she's pretty dehydrated. Could be flu...doctor think it's stress related. Said a few days of TLC might do her good. She asked me to let you know she wouldn't be able to keep her appointment this morning."

"I would think not! Which hospital is she in? Can I see her?"

"Don't know why not. She's in University Hospital. Just ask at the desk for her room number."

❦

"Are you family?" the information clerk enquired, her gaze taking in the young man with the armful of roses.

"Soon, I hope," he answered cheerfully.

"Miss Stevenson is on the second floor; you might just enquire at the nursing station."

Wonder why they won't give me her room number. Is she that sick?

"Are you next of kin?" the nurse looked up from her chart.

"Not just yet," he joked.

"I'm sorry, we have orders that only next of kin...."

"Can I ask why? Is she that sick?"

"I'm sorry I can't answer that. Dr. Bates has ordered complete bed rest...restricted visiting."

"Who wants to see her?" the voice came from behind him.

"Hello, Doctor, I'm Brett Walker. I think Leanne would like to see me...."

"No doubt." He smiled, eyeing the armful of pink roses. "I don't see why not...keep it short."

She lay sleeping...her face almost as white as the hospital linen...one arm imprisoned by a blood-pressure cuff, the other taped up with intravenous. A blood-pressure machine monitored her on one side, and she wore a small oxygen clip in her nose.

He watched her for a few minutes. *How did she get so bad so fast? She didn't seem sick last night. Whatever could have happened since then?* He busied himself filling the vase with water and arranging the roses, as quietly as he could.

He looked up to see her eyes following him. "Hello, Brett. Nice of you to come. Sorry I didn't make our meeting this morning."

"Kitten," he murmured, kissing her forehead. "Whatever happened?"

"Don't know. Just had a hard time breathing...lost my breakfast...then my balance. Doctor thinks it's stress related."

"Well, you've had enough of it to last for a few years. They told me not to linger, but is there anything I can get for you...have sent up?"

"Don't think so...but it's good to see you."

"Don't know if they'll let me back in...since I'm not next of kin. I'd like to remedy that real soon," he finished with a grin.

"The roses are gorgeous." She smiled.

"Like you...except that right now they have a lot more colour. Whatever did we do to you? Were you feeling this bad last night?"

"No...but I may have been running on nervous energy. Can't believe how terrible I felt after I went to bed. Had quite a time trying to sleep...kept seeing Lonnie. Then, this morning I guess I just lost it. Maybe I was coming out of shock, or something."

"Just relax now, kitten. You need to get better. Don't worry about your exams; we'll do okay." He smoothed back her hair and kissed her forehead. "Don't forget that I love you. Promise?"

She smiled and nodded.

"See you this evening…if they let me in."

※

He was pleased to see that her face had regained a slight flesh tone, when he returned after supper. Maybe it was the pink pyjamas; Sherry must have brought some of her things, he decided.

"Thank you for being with me the other night," she whispered. "Guess I didn't have a clue what I was facing." She shuddered. "Is he out on bail?"

"Yes, he is, Lee. But I plan to come back with you while you write your exams. I promised to help you study. You may not need my protection, but it may give you a little more peace of mind, so you can get your thoughts around your exams."

"That's awfully good of you, Brett, but way too much to ask. You have a practice to…."

"Shhh, never mind that. I've worked it out with Dave; he and Becky will keep the lid on till we get back."

"We?"

"We think you should come home for the holidays as soon as exams are over. Actually, Dave has arranged for a condo at Blue Mountain for the week following Christmas. That boy seems determined to teach me to ski." He smiled. "Besides, it will be refreshing for all of us. He says your family has done this for years."

"Yes, except the last two," she said, remembering. "Sounds like fun!"

"Good. Then we need to get you better and out of here. Are you eating?"

She smiled. "Trying. They don't cook like the Crock and Block, or Sammy's, or even the Swiss Chalet. In fact, I think McDonald's would stand head and shoulders above."

"Shall I send for some chicken and ribs?"

"No, but I'll look forward to doing that again some time. I really enjoyed that evening...the food...the studying...right up until Lonnie...."

"I'm glad, Lee." He wondered how she would react if she knew about her neighbour's phone call to Dave...that she had seen Lonnie's car go by twice in the last couple of hours; that his accompanying her was more than an act of love—though it was that—it was a decision that he and Dave had made to give her the added protection and peace of mind she would need in order to get through her exams.

"What will happen next semester? Will I need to transfer to Western?"

"Let's take it one day at a time. The Lord still knows the way through the wilderness."

He bent and kissed her nose. "Good to see you don't need oxygen anymore. How can I steal a kiss...?" He touched his lips lightly to hers. He noticed that she allowed his kiss, but did not respond. *Patience, Walker, patience*, he told himself.

"Is it still Thursday?" she asked. "Seems like I've been here such a long time. Doctor says if I behave he may let me out Saturday morning. Sure would be nice to go to church here again...it's been a while. Do you ever see Brody's folks in church?"

"All the time. They're back together. Actually, they both gave a little talk a few weeks back; she asked the forgiveness of the people for the deception. He told about his conversion and his desire to live for Christ. I was really quite moved by what they said."

"I'm so glad," she smiled, "so glad! So good to hear that the Lord is alive and well."

"My little social worker," he teased.

"So...are you going to tell me what happened to Tony Cortez? Dave said...."

"Tony and I go back a long way...nearly 20 years. Don't think you have time or energy to hear all that tonight."

"That will do! That's about the fourth time you've found an excuse. I have loads of time; energy...well?"

159

He hesitated as if struggling with himself, then began slowly, "Well, I guess I told you my mom died when I was ten. I think she had breast cancer…at least that's what I think they told me. My dad had Lou Gehrig's disease for a number of years but had been able to get along pretty well. He was an investment broker. After Mom died, he tried to look after me and keep the business going, but he started to go downhill quite quickly. Maybe the lack of will to carry on had something to do with it.

"Finally, he found a housekeeper. By this time I was about twelve and did much of the housework…some cooking…laundry. I also had a paper route that kept me pretty busy part of each evening.

"Dad was spending more and more time in the wheelchair and had his lawyer over more and more often. Guess he was preparing for his demise but they figured I was too young to be told…or included in the plans.

"I came home from school one day to find this woman taking over the kitchen…the house. Dad introduced her as Mrs. Rosita Cortez, our new housekeeper. He outlined how much easier it would be for me…that I wouldn't have to do so much…and on and on. I was devastated. I didn't mind looking after Dad. I just wanted him all to myself. I couldn't bear the thought that my mom was being replaced with this…this…."

"Oh, Brett." Her eyes were wide and sympathetic.

"Dad deteriorated quite quickly after that. Guess he knew he would need more help than I could give him. We had a nurse come in every day to check on him, bathe him, give him his meds and whatever. Mrs. Cortez looked after the house pretty well, but she always seemed so secretive where Dad was concerned. Wouldn't let me see him. I would sneak in and cuddle with him when she went for groceries.

"Pretty soon he couldn't talk intelligibly and I wasn't always sure what he was trying to communicate.

"One day I came home and there were about a dozen people in the house, all dressed in dark suits and white shirts. I thought Dad had died. However, it seemed to be much more festive than that…flowers all over the place. Rosita was all dressed up, standing beside Dad's bed, holding his hand. Suddenly, I realized what had happened. She had married Dad. Whether he knew what had happened, I wasn't sure. I ran from the house and crawled into the dog house with my big collie, Laddie. He seemed all that I had left in the world."

"Oh, Brett," she said again, as tears slid down her face.

"I tried to think what to do and finally I decided I'd better visit Mr. Benton, Dad's lawyer, and ask him what was going on. He was some surprised and called on Dad at once. He quickly ascertained that Dad had not sanctioned such a thing. Someone else had signed for him, and she was already signing her name Rosita Cortez Walker.

"Fortunately Dad had left everything to me. He had put some annuities in my name that couldn't be cashed in till I was eighteen, twenty, twenty-two and twenty-four. Mr. Benton explained that there was plenty of money to look after me, but I really had no one to look after me from day to day.

"Things moved pretty fast after that. I came home from my paper route one day to find a big hulking kid, probably about eighteen, sitting in the kitchen, having cookies and hot chocolate. Rosita introduced him as my big brother. He grinned and sneered all at the same time. He took over the guest room and enjoyed helping himself to anything and everything that was mine, including Laddie. He was cruel to both of us, and Laddie would often growl when he saw him coming. He broke most of my stuff and laughed when I was distressed.

"Every second Friday evening was payday for my paper route. Course I couldn't deposit it till Monday morning so I always had it over the weekend. I'll never know how he knew I got paid, but he simply took it away from me. His mother watched without comment. The next day he showed up with the switchblade…the one that killed the night watchman."

Leanne gasped.

"Now he had a new method of torture. A few times I noticed blood in Laddie's fur and I knew he was tormenting him, but I came upon him unexpectedly one day…he was holding the knife to Laddie's nose and watching him back away growling in fear. I didn't stop to think what he might do with the knife; I just grabbed him from behind, spun him around and broke his nose with one blow. My fist hurt for a week, and all the while I grinned. Anyway, the knife went flying. I was too concerned about the dog to go after it…too bad! He fled to his mother, blood flying everywhere.

"The next Friday night when I came from school a social worker was waiting for me and took me to a home for troubled teens. Whether my dad actually understood what was happening, I'm not sure. Rosita had apparently explained that I was quite violent and that my dad was too sick to be disturbed. I never saw him alive again. He died a few months later and I wouldn't have known had not Mr. Benton found out and got in touch with Social Services. He was absolutely outraged at what had happened and took me to the funeral. Afterward, they moved me into their home to live with them."

"Were you able to get Laddie?"

"No. They said he became vicious and had to be destroyed."

"How dreadful! What happened to your home?"

"The lawyer couldn't prove that she hadn't married Dad, so she got first rights. However, as soon as I told him and he found out about the mock wedding, he quickly borrowed against the house in Dad's name and put it into an annuity for me. She eventually lost the house since she couldn't make the payments. She got a good sum from his bank accounts but Tony just sucked her dry. He got a new Ferrari right off the bat. That would probably have dried up the vat pretty fast."

"How did you get along with your new foster parents? Were you happy there?"

"They really tried to look after me well. They were well up in years…their kids were grown and had kids my age. They came over to play sometimes. I got a good foundation in ethics, education, good sportsmanship, all that sort of thing. I had lots of opportunity to socialize…learn to dance…sports…music. They were sure Mom and Dad would have wanted the best for me. I got my desire to go into law from Mr. Benton. Guess I thought maybe I could set the world right if I was a lawyer. So, the Lord turned the tables and gave me a really wonderful home, though I didn't realize what a gift it was while I was growing up; I was lonely for my parents, and hungering for revenge on

Tony and Rosita. I'm sure my drive to compete in sports and academics was fuelled by my desire for revenge."

"Did the Bentons have faith in God?"

"They went to church regularly, but I refused. Guess my anger at the Cortez family was really anger at God…for allowing such people to live…and to come into my life."

"Big decision for a pre-teen to make."

"No kidding. Pretty far-reaching consequences. Good thing Mom had led me to the Lord when I was seven or eight, and He never let me go."

She squeezed his hand. "Do I gather that Tony has had his trial?"

"Actually, he changed his plea to guilty, and I spoke to his sentencing. He got ten years without parole."

"Did you think it was just?"

"More than fair. I asked for a psychiatric assessment, counseling, a chance to get an education. More than he deserves for all the evils he has inflicted on young boys, and society in general."

"You are quite a guy, Brett Walker." She spoke with deep emotion. "When did you decide that getting even was not the way to go?"

"About the same time you came into my life. The more I watched you, the more my hunger grew to get my life in order. I knew I needed forgiveness for my attitude toward Tony and Rosita. I had started to hate the sight of a Latin face. Bitterness grows. But I hated to give up the idea of revenge. Each time I saw that he was back in jail, I felt smug. Then this little *social worker* type came along…."

Her eyes were warm and soft as he bent toward her. She slipped her arm around his neck and pulled him close as his lips met hers.

"I love you, kitten."

"I love you, too, Brett Walker. I've loved you for a long time; I just didn't know who you were."

CHAPTER TWENTY-NINE

"Can I call you *Auntie Lee?*" the blonde four-year-old asked as they enjoyed Auntie Sherry's wedding album. "I know that Sherry is really my cousin, but she doesn't mind if I call her *auntie*. And I call Mr. Walker *Uncle Brett*. It's not so hard to say."

Lee smiled as the bright little girl chattered on.

"When I grow up I'm going to be a bride, like Auntie Sherry. Isn't she beautiful? What are you going to be when you grow up, Auntie Lee?" She finally paused for breath and looked at Lee.

"I'm not really sure; maybe I'll be a social worker...." She waited for a reaction from behind the newspaper covering the man in the armchair.

"When Auntie Lee grows up, she's going to marry me," came the reply.

A well-aimed cushion sent the paper sailing out of his hands, but the child seemed not to notice as her ringlets bobbed in surprise. "Oh, really, Auntie Lee, and I can be your flower girl! See how pretty I was for Auntie Sherry's wedding...and I already have my dress."

"Oh, sweetheart, Uncle Brett is making jokes; he's a rascal...."

"But Auntie Lee loves rascals, twelve on a scale of one...." He ducked as another pillow sailed past his head.

"And besides," Lee continued, "it may take Auntie Lee a long time to grow up."

"How long?" from the armchair.

"Not more than twenty-five years or so."

"Dinner's on," Dave called.

"Guess what?" the precocious child continued as they sat down to eat. "Uncle Brett is going to marry Auntie Lee as soon as she grows up…in just twenty-five years or so…and I'm going to be her flower girl…cause I already have my dress."

Laughter burst forth from aunts, uncles, and grandparents; Brett smirked as Lee gave him an *I'll tend to you later* look.

"Well, that's quite a story," Dave started after they had asked the Lord's blessing. "Any details you'd care to share with us?"

"But Auntie Lee is gonna be a social worker first," the child added as an afterthought.

"We'll keep you posted…annual bulletins…twenty-five years is a while…." Brett looked at Lee, his smirk still in place.

"I think I'd like one of those nice warm rolls," Lee tried a change of subject, much to everyone's amusement.

"So where will you be articling, Lee?" from Grandma Wilson.

"It's in the process of being decided," she offered, thankful for the change of topic. "I have another very full semester and a lot of exams before I get that far. I'm really looking forward to being done."

❧

He sat at his desk, hurriedly finishing his final draft on the computer. Lee was due any minute and he would be done just in time. He heard the door open and close and turned with a smile…just in time to see Rhonda perch on the corner of his desk. Crossing her bare legs, she leaned forward, nearly draping him in her long blonde hair.

"Now, big boy, do we have something to discuss…?"

He was speechless for a moment, then spotted the door closing gently. "Lee," he called as he jumped up, nearly dumping Rhonda on the floor. "Lee, come in." He ran to the outer office; she was not there. Becky was not at her desk…out to the elevator…it was somewhere between floors.

Rhonda waited…amusement playing around the corners of her mouth. "Do you always make that much fuss over her?"

165

"You bet!" Then, making no effort to veil his disgust, he turned to her. "Rhonda, I have asked you for the last time not to darken the door of these offices. Today I will be charging you with harassment, and taking out a restraining order." He moved past her and strode down the hall to the offices of the Hansen group. Much to the chagrin of the senior partner, Ron Hansen, he repeated his promise. Rhonda slunk past him as she was summoned to Ron's office.

"Becky, have you seen Lee?" he asked as he swung through the door and found her now at her desk. "Yes, she's in with Dave…waiting for you, I think she said."

He tapped at the door and walked in. Two sets of eyes looked up at him…each with a question. "Will you come in?" he addressed Lee. "Maybe you'd like to join us too, Dave."

"In answer to your question," he began as they took seats near the desk, "I did not have an appointment with Rhonda Fleming. I intend to follow through on my promise to charge her with harassment and get a restraining order. If there are no more questions…." He looked from one to the other.

"Thank you, Brett," she said with a slight smile.

"And thank you for waiting, Lee. Guess it must have been a bit of a surprise to find her draped all over my desk. It was a surprise to me, too. I had been working on the computer, when I turned around expecting you…there she was. Sorry, I didn't get the restraining order the first time I mentioned it. I'll remedy that today."

Lee enjoyed going over the articles with Brett and her brother. They had carefully outlined requirements, responsibilities, opportunities, salary; no mention of office space. She decided not to ask. When they completed the presentation, she knew it was the only place she really wanted to be.

"Do we have a luncheon date?" Brett asked Lee, as Dave headed for home.

"Sounds good to me."

"So what do you think? Do we have a deal?" he asked as the waiter disappeared with their order.

She smiled. "I'd be a fool not to get on the wagon with you two…." She paused, then added, "But you know I make important decisions very slowly. I think I need some advice from someone outside the firm…and…well…I think I owe it to Mr. Foster to hear what he has to say."

She could sense his disappointment as he reached for her hand. "Thank you, Lee. Thank you for considering us. Can I ask who you intend to seek advice from?"

"I haven't made up my mind on that score. I'm sure Uncle Ben would like to be consulted and will have a very definite opinion. Other than that…."

"That wretched Foster! He never misses an opportunity," the retired judge growled as he sat back in his favourite chair. "Tell me, how much did he offer you?"

"More than twice what Brett and Dave…."

"I thought so! Just like him to see a chance like that. He knows jolly well that you're a very capable lawyer…not to mention the clients that will follow you. He can well afford to pay double that amount and still make money. I'm glad Dave didn't take his bait…hope you don't either. He might be a good friend of mine…but he better watch himself when it comes to my little girl!"

Leanne smiled. He would never see her as anything but his little girl…though he did concede that she was a capable lawyer. She would wait now until the end of the semester; it would give her time to think the situation over one more time.

The week flew by. She felt so much better. It really was a good idea to come to London to get ready for her exams. With Brett coaching her in the evenings, she felt confident and prepared for next week. She was comfortable, too, that he would stay with her till she finished.

CHAPTER THIRTY

Even back in Toronto, thoughts of Lonnie moved to the back burner...at least until she picked up her back issue of *The Star*. Headlines informed her that dozens of students, past and present, had phoned in complaints about him, a number had charged him with sexual assault, several with rape. That he was out on bail seemed preposterous. *Guess money and influence speak*, she mused. "Dean Strauss has been temporarily suspended, pending an investigation," she read to Brett.

"High time," he responded as he carried her luggage to her room.

"I'm so glad you're here; what ever would I do all by myself?" She moved to give him a hug and he held her close.

"I intend to take you to your exams, you know. I can work in the library."

"Do you really think he would still try something?"

"Just a precaution. After all, you not only successfully fended off his advances, you are the one who exposed him, taped his conversations and phone calls and gave them to the dean and the police. He's plenty mad. He seems to have a very obsessive-compulsive personality. I just want to be here in case he goes off the edge."

She turned on her answering machine. No phone calls from Lonnie—that's a plus—a call from Walter Strauss, the former Dean Strauss, asking her to meet him for coffee. He had left his number.

"Shall I meet him?" she asked.

"Only if he doesn't mind my being there."

She made the arrangements—tomorrow at 4:00, right after her exam.

⊚⊚⊚

He rose and extended his hand to her, then to Brett. She noted with relief that he had picked a very private booth.

"Miss Stevenson…Leanne, I owe you an apology…more than that I need to ask your forgiveness for putting you at risk the way I did. In my own defense, I must tell you that I had no idea he had resorted to threats…no idea of the magnitude of his preying on students. I must admit to being quite overwhelmed with the reports coming out in the morning papers. Reporters are having a heyday…."

They sat silently; it was not what they had expected to hear from him.

"I don't believe Leanne was intending to press charges against you…or the university, Mr. Strauss," Brett offered.

"I am, of course, relieved to know that, but…well…it goes beyond that with me. I am a man of strong faith…guess I have always prided myself in doing the right thing by others. I am ashamed that I didn't protect a student as vulnerable as Leanne…especially when she came to me…confided in me…collected all the evidence. I must ask you again, Leanne…do you have it in your heart to forgive me?"

"Yes. You are forgiven for your part in this. I must say that I am sorry for the way it turned out. My brother had been in town…heard the threat on my answering machine. Lonnie intended to spend Tuesday night with me…with or without my permission. Dave was aghast. He discussed it with Brett. They decided I needed protection, so Brett came. My study group met until 11:00. Lonnie was waiting. Of course, he didn't know that Brett was with me, but he tried to break down the door, then started on the window. By this time, the neighbour had called 9-1-1. I called in, too, but the police were already at the door. There was really little else we could do," she finished.

"I appreciate knowing what happened. Perhaps it has all turned out for the best. I thought many times of confronting Lonnie, but it would

169

have been his word against the student. When it came to you, I just thought he needed time to show his colours...so that he would be removed from his exalted position...he was seeking tenure. In my foolishness I put you at considerable risk. I am truly sorry."

They rose to go.

"Am I right in surmising that there is more than a client-counselor relationship here?"

"We are very special friends." She smiled at Brett.

"Guess I wondered when he comes to stay...." His face reddened.

"Leanne has two guest rooms; I happily occupy one of them."

"Thank you for sharing that with me. It's none of my business, of course, but I have gotten to know Leanne...she has a very high standard...guess I would have been disappointed...." He fumbled for words.

"If that were the case, Mr. Strauss...I would be disappointed, too...in myself."

"I'll need to pick up some milk, Brett, and fresh cream for our coffee," she said as he opened the door. "Should have gotten that on the way home."

"I'll slip down to the Quik Mart; just be sure to keep the door locked." She looked up at the seriousness in his voice.

"Honestly, Brett, he wouldn't try anything at this time of day...it's hardly dark."

"Don't take any chances, kitten. I'll be right back."

CHAPTER THIRTY-ONE

Lee isn't taking this situation nearly seriously enough, he mused as he headed to the small confectionery. *Course she doesn't know he's been cruising her neighbourhood...maybe she needs to be told.*

Something caught his eye in the oncoming traffic...could it be? Were his eyes playing tricks on him or was it really Lonnie? His hair stood in whisps like a madman...he was unshaven...in a different vehicle...it couldn't be...please...no. How would he get turned around in this traffic? He froze thinking of the implications. *Best call Lee and let her know...make sure she doesn't open the door for him.*

His heart hammered against the walls of his chest as he heard the steady *beep beep* that told him she was on the phone. *Oh, God*, he prayed, as he quickly dialled 9-1-1. *Better to be wrong and thought a fool, than to be right and do nothing.*

"Sorry, Dave, can you hold for a sec? Brett must have forgotten something." She laid the phone aside and scurried to slide back the bolt in answer to his knock.

"Well, Miss Lee, we meet at last," the wild-eyed professor sneered, "and without an armed guard."

She moved quickly to close the door, as he pushed his way in and made a grab for her. She noticed he had something small in his hand...a cord....

*Oh, God, he's going to strangle me...help...*she prayed as he flexed the small cord between his hands and came toward her. She moved back and forth, sidestepping him, then suddenly he lunged, missed her and sent the tri-lamp crashing to the floor. She screamed.

On the other end of the line, her brother listened in horror as her attacker swore, yelled and threatened; thunder and lightning erupted around the room. He buzzed Becky to call 9-1-1 in Toronto while he stayed on the line. Suddenly there was a crash in his ear as Lee's phone hit the floor and went dead.

"Oh, God," the young lawyer prayed, "you know how totally helpless I am to help my sister; only You can deliver her from this madman."

Thank you, God. Brett breathed as he swung through a small break in the opposing traffic and turned around. His mind still bore the imprint of the man…a maniac!

She was faster than her adversary; round and round they went, chairs, end-tables, lamps, pictures askew. She backed against the armchair; he sneered; he had her cornered. She jumped over the top and pushed it at him. He swore as she moved for the door. Suddenly she tripped on the lamp cord, he lunged and his cord was around her neck. She struggled desperately as she cried out to God for help. She would remember it afterward as being an involuntary action, but her foot found a strategic target. He doubled over, screaming obscenities and holding his groin. She dashed for the door and collided with a white-faced Brett as he ran up the steps.

"Thank God, you're okay."

He moved to block the door, as Lonnie scrambled to remove himself from the scene. "Now, Lonnie, let's just take it easy." Brett's voice was remarkably calm. "There's no place to run; my car is blocking you in."

"I've had enough from you two," he yelled, waving his cord and uttering more obscenities as he staggered threateningly toward Brett.

Brett backed away as two police cars stopped at the curb. "Just take it easy, Lonnie; these nice gentlemen have come to take care of you for a while."

Cameras began to click, and Brett realized that reporters seemed to have come out of nowhere. Lonnie's arrest would be well documented. He shuddered as he thought of Lee trying to write her final exam tomorrow. They would need to talk to the university...after all, they were responsible for letting this situation get this far out of hand.

"We'll need to get some statements," the officer reminded them.

"I think she needs to stop at the hospital and get this looked after first. My guess is that she'll need a sedative once the shock wears off. If you care to follow us, I can give you a statement; Lee will have to give hers later. We'll definitely be down to press charges."

"Why did you come back?" she asked Brett as they drove.

"I saw him heading your way...took me a few seconds to realize it was him...his hair...whiskers...he was in a different vehicle. Then I couldn't find a place to turn around, so that took me almost to the end of the crescent. By that time I was in a bit of a panic, sending up SOSs that God would protect you. I know how trusting you are, Lee...." He looked at her. "You have a hard time imagining that anyone would really try to do you in...even after Lonnie's last escapade."

"I am sorry, Brett. I thought it was you...that maybe you'd forgotten something. If I had just looked through the safety glass, I would never have opened for him. Was it you who called the police?"

"Soon as I recognized him I tried to call you...got a busy signal. I panicked and called 9-1-1. Fortunately, they knew about him from before so I didn't have to do a lot of explaining. I just told them that I saw him heading toward your place and that he looked like a wild man. Thank God they got right on it...we would have had a time trying to control him...like having a maniac on our hands."

"Oh, I'd better call Dave. I was on the phone with him and I just laid the receiver down so I could open the door for you. He must have heard the whole thing...at least until Lonnie sent the phone to its uncertain end."

"However did you get away on him?"

She laughed shakily. "Well, we were struggling. He had the cord around my neck and I knew I wouldn't be long for this world, and I was flailing about, crying out to God for deliverance, when suddenly I just kicked him. Guess I'm not the only one who should see a doctor. I suspect he may need a little medical attention…don't think he'll be bothering any students for a few weeks."

"Lee Stevenson…you little hell cat; no wonder he was holding himself…all bent over. And I thought you needed my protection!" He chuckled.

"Any chance he might try to charge me with assault?"

He chuckled again. "Who knows. My guess is that he'll be too embarrassed to have that hit the media. On the other hand, Hencken and Mears may use it as part of their defense…he tried to strangle you to protect himself…."

She took his cell phone and quickly dialled her brother. "Hello, Dave, sorry to put you through all that! I'm still alive. Brett rescued me…again!"

"Lee…Lee." His voice caught. "Thank God you're safe. I've never felt so helpless in my whole life. That guy needs to be put away for life. Are you okay?"

"Some batters and bruises…pretty bad rope burn around my neck…nothing as bad as my living room got."

"So I heard."

Brett reached across and took the phone. "Don't let her kid you that I rescued her, Dave. She had that poor mutt on his knees howling in pain when I arrived; he won't be harassing any little girls for quite some time." He chuckled. "We're on our way to emergency; Lee will need something when she comes out of shock. Don't know what will happen with her exams; we'll keep you posted."

"Honestly, Brett. I'm not looking forward to having this thing hanging over my head…trying to write my exam and feeling like the students and staff are whispering, 'that's her…you know the one that Hencken….' They didn't know it was me before…now our pictures are going to be smeared all over the morning papers. I don't think I can cope." She covered her face with her hands.

"That's why we're going to see a doctor. You'll need a sedative…something to settle you down."

"I can't take that stuff. I have to write an exam tomorrow."

"They'll have to cut you some slack, Lee. I doubt they'll give me any static. Do you know what percent of your final mark this exam is worth?"

"I think it's 20 percent."

"So basically you've already passed?"

"Yeah. Marks for my course work are enough to get me through. It's just that I had counted on…..." She was shaking now as they pulled up to the emergency unit.

"I know, kitten." He put his arms around her. "You had planned on pulling off top marks, and that's precisely why they need to accommodate you. Either they change the time and date of your exam so you can cope, or they give you the marks that they know you'll make. I doubt they'll give me any argument."

"You don't think I'll be able to write tomorrow."

"Let's wait and see. I'd sure hate for you to try when your mind's a blank. Lee, you owe it to yourself…and they owe it to you…to let you do your best. If they want you back next semester…want you to graduate here…."

She struggled to swing her legs out of the passenger seat, then cried out in pain as her left one refused to budge. He ran for a wheelchair and lifted her carefully. She caught sight of herself as he pushed her past the huge glass doors.

"I look like a one-woman war zone," she muttered, noting her hair askew, her face bruised and scratched. Fortunately, her jacket covered the torn shirt and the black and blue bruises on her arms and neck.

❦

"It's been one awful night," she said as she sank gratefully into the soft pillows on her own bed. Her leg had been x-rayed and the swollen, twisted knee fitted with a supporting brace and bandage. She would have to keep off it for at least a week. "Is the nightmare over, Brett, or is it just beginning?"

"If I have to be honest, kitten, it's both. At least you won't have to worry about Lonnie showing up in unexpected places. They'll probably charge him with attempted murder…that should keep him under lock and key for a while. You know you'll have to testify, and I certainly intend to. After that, we will need to press charges. A number of the students have talked to me about it already. Maybe a *class action* lawsuit would be in order. If that's the case, Dave and I would have to face off against the senior Hencken and Mears."

"Oh, Brett." Her face was still white, her voice a little slurred with the sedative taking effect.

"It'll be okay, kitten. You know both of us love a challenge. Now you need a really good sleep. I'll talk to the university about your exam in the morning. Good thing you have only one left to write." Then taking her hand, he thanked God for keeping them through all the challenges of the day, and for whatever the future would hold.

Chapter Thirty-Two

She heard the soft murmur of voices as she lay in that delicious state between wakefulness and sleep. Dave and Sherry were up early...probably stuffing the turkey and getting it in the oven. Christmas dinner would be around one o'clock. The big dining room table would be filled with guests—Sherry's folks and her brother Bob, Judge Ben and Aunt Maude; Sherry's cousins would be coming; the little blonde Lisa with the ringlets and the bridesmaid's dress. *Won't she be surprised that I've grown up some.* She smiled to herself.

She looked forward to the day with a mixture of emotion. Thoughts of Christmases past crowded in. She remembered her mom...getting the lovely mink stole from her dad...the look they exchanged; twenty-four hours later she lay in the morgue, her husband hanging between life and death. And last year...Dad on oxygen most of the time, confined to his wheelchair or his recliner.

But today...today would be too special to dwell on the pain of the past; better to dwell on the immediate past...like last evening with Brett. He had made filet mignon, baked potatoes, string beans, a variety of veggies and salad. One of their favorite meals. What fun to be there alone with him...dreaming...wondering if she would live there with him one day...*Mrs. Brett Walker*....

They had danced—slowly to accommodate her still-healing knee. She would never forget what happened next.

He pulled her onto his lap as they shared the love seat. "Do you love me, kitten?" He turned her face to look into her eyes.

177

"You know I do."

"What do you love about me?" His eyes searched her face.

"Oh…everything!"

"What does everything look like?"

"Like you," she said, running her fingers gently down his face…his chin…his neck. "I love the way you look…your masculinity…the way you dress…the way you walk…the way you love me…care for me…hold me…kiss me. I love the way you want to please the Lord in your business and personal life. I think we share many of the same values…."

She broke off as he pulled her close, her face in his neck. When he spoke next, his voice was husky. "Do you love me enough to make it a lifetime contract, Lee? Will you marry me?"

"Oh…Brett," she whispered, her eyes seeking his. "Is that what you really want?"

"You must know by now…." His eyes looked into hers as he nodded.

"Then…yes…I'll marry you."

He reached for her hand and slipped his ring on her finger. "Forever and always, my beautiful kitten," he murmured.

They had laughed and kissed and talked. He wanted to get married tomorrow…she said it would take longer than that to get ready. He suggested two weeks…before she went back to school. She insisted she couldn't learn to be a wife and complete her studies. Around and around they went until they finally decided on June 1. She smiled, remembering that he thought he should surely die of anticipation before then.

He wanted to announce it at dinner today. He would do it in his own unique way, she was sure. She slipped her lovely ring back into its box. She would put it on just before dinner. What fun!

It takes me back to my childhood, Lee thought as she surveyed the scene before her. *The tree shimmering with lights, tinsel, trinkets, gifts—icicles hanging from the windows.*

Sherry read the Christmas story and Dave led in a prayer giving thanks to God, before they began the fun of discovery.

Brett was overwhelmed with the new skis from Dave and Sherry, and the ski outfit from Lee. "Tried to get one that matched mine," she explained, "not that I'll be able to ski anyway, but maybe another time."

He had bought her a knitted suit of fine British wool. She gasped as she lifted it from the package.

Oo's and ah's continued as each package was opened—china and crystal for Sherry…to match her sets; a generous bonus for Dave from Brett; Lee's favorite perfume from Sherry.

So this is how a real family celebrates Christmas morning! Brett thought. He sat quietly watching the excitement. *And in just a few months I'm going to belong; I'm going to belong to this family. Guess I'll need to get Dave aside and ask him for Lee's hand. Wonder what he'll say. He seems to approve of our relationship…at least lately.*

The girls headed to the kitchen as the men began restoring order in anticipation of the invasion of guests.

"Dave, can we sit for a minute?" Brett asked as they finished with the paper.

"Good idea. I'll just grab us a coffee."

He doesn't seem to be suspecting anything, Brett mused, as they settled into chairs by the fire. "Dave," he began. The younger man looked up at the seriousness in his voice. "I have asked Leanne to marry me. Do I have your permission?"

Her brother sat for a few moments as his face changed colour a few times. "Do you have *her* permission?" he asked.

"I do," Brett assured him.

"Then I guess I better give you mine." Her brother smiled.

"Thank you, Dave," he managed before the door burst open and cousins began pouring in. *Looks like I didn't ask any too soon.*

⊚⊚⊚

"I do have an announcement to make," Brett began as plates were being pushed back and overly satiated guests contemplated dessert. "I mentioned a few weeks ago that I would give annual updates as to

179

Auntie Lee's progress on her 25-year program. It seems, however, that in the latter part of the semester she matured so quickly...." he looked down at her and grinned, "that she has been able to fast-forward on her agenda." He enjoyed having everyone's attention now, and lifting Lee's left hand, he continued. "We have set the date for June 1."

Amid the cheers and congratulations, a tiny voice was heard, "What's happening, Mommie? Is Auntie Lee going to marry Uncle Brett?"

"Yes, honey."

"Oh, Auntie Lee, will you hurry? Mommie says my dress won't fit pretty soon."

❦

"Mr. Foster would like you to go right in." The receptionist smiled as Lee approached her desk..

He rose quickly and extended his hand. "Miss Lee...Miss Lee, how good to see you! I trust your holiday season was a happy one. Sit down. Sit down."

She nodded and returned his smile. *No point in prolonging this; may as well get it over with*, she assured herself. "Mr. Foster," she began, as he waited expectantly. "I wanted to let you know that I have made up my mind...I have decided to article with Brett Walker."

"Yes...yes. I was afraid of that...with your brother there and all. Are you sure this is wise, Lee? I am prepared to offer you more money...I am ready to negotiate."

He paused as she raised her hand. "It's a done deal, Mr. Foster. I've accepted a life-time contract from Brett as of June 1." Slowly she drew off her glove and extended her left hand across the desk. The lovely ring sparkled up at him.

He drew a long breath, then swallowed before he spoke. "Well, I'll be. I should have guessed. I thought there was something going for a while there, then there was Lonnie...and Brett was such a committed bachelor.... Well, I'll be. I guess congratulations are in order."

He extended his hand as he spoke.

"There never was a *Lonnie*, Mr. Foster. That was all in his imagination."

"I should have known when Brett got so riled when I asked him about it. He's a determined rascal—goes after what he wants. Looks like he's won this one fair and square. He's a good man. All the best to you both."

She smiled as she rose. "You are right, Mr. Foster. He is a good man...goes after what he wants. He didn't spare the horses, as they say."

She was still smiling as she stopped at the office to bid farewell to her beloved before she started back for Toronto and her final semester.

Chapter Thirty-Three

"I have to see you, Lee. I'm in town and I'd like to see you before I leave. Tried to get you on the cell, but guess you must have been in class. Give me a call, okay?"

She turned off her answering machine and quickly dialled his cell number. His voice sounded both serious and urgent.

"Come for supper, sweetheart. I have it in the oven," she assured him.

Her heart thumped loudly as he sat across from her in the family room. "I'm sorry, kitten, I'm afraid I have some rather sobering news." She noted that he looked haggard...stressed.

Oh, dear, God, she prayed, *don't let it be that we can't get married.*

"Come, sit with me," she invited, taking his hand, "it makes it easier to talk."

"I guess I thought this ugly thing would go away," he struggled for words, "but...."

Her thoughts flew wildly...what could he be talking about...was it still Rhonda? She tried to calm her emotions...to wait quietly....

"You know I've been struggling...." He leaned forward, covering his face with his hands.

"Brett...sweetheart...tell me. Let me help...." She slipped her arms around him as he shook with sobs.

"I...I...didn't really know what the problem was...guess I'd just numbed it out. The counselor says it was probably too painful for a kid to endure, so my mind just blanked it out. He says you need to know about it...."

He took a number of deep breaths in an attempt to gain composure. "I...I..." he tried again, "kitten, I'm sorry. I don't know what this means for our marriage...."

"Can you tell me about it, dearest? Is it too painful to talk about?"

"You know I've been having horrible dreams...nightmares...in the last year. They drove me to distraction." She nodded. "I'd wake up fighting, pillows flying, blankets twisted...bed trashed.... Doesn't sound too good for a marriage."

She chuckled softly. "You got that right. So...?"

He took several more deep and shaky breaths, then continued, "I never could remember much about my time in the group home. Guess I had just blocked it out of my conscious mind. Over the last few months I've been working on trying to remember. At first I couldn't even remember the rooms, especially the bedrooms. Gradually I was able to place the kitchen, the living room, and finally...." He paused, unable to go on.

She waited.

"The counselor, Dr. Hayes, questioned me about the furniture. Eventually, I began to put the pieces in place. The bedroom was a complete blank for months. Last night it suddenly came to me...like my mind just opened up...and I saw the inside of the bedroom and I knew what had happened there."

Her arms tightened around him as he tried desperately to control his emotions.

"I'm...not sure I can tell you about this," he whispered.

"Yes, you can, dearest. We can share your pain together."

"There were three other boys in the same room...older than me. Two of them were brothers and they did unimaginable things to each other. I was a lot smaller than any one of them, and was helpless against the three of them. They tortured me endlessly at night. I tried to protect myself with my pillow and blankets, and of course, it was only a source of amusement to them that I tried to fend them off. They threatened me if I told. Said the houseparents wouldn't do anything and they'd really fix me."

"Oh, how horrible! You poor little kid!"

"That's what I feel like when I wake from one of the nightmares…like a little kid…scared and cowering…exhausted…the bed a mess…."

They held each other quietly. She could feel the thump of his heart, along with her own.

"Does Dr. Hayes…." She paused, then tried again. "Does he think there will be healing now that you know what it is?"

"He thinks so, but…says that time will tell."

"So…are you afraid?" She looked at him, unable to go on.

"To get married?" he finished for her.

She nodded.

"I was afraid before…didn't know why…just kind of a nameless fear. At least I know now. I guess I'm wondering…we need to talk about…." He hesitated.

"About what, sweetheart?"

"Whether you still want to marry me…whether we should postpone the wedding until we're sure…."

"You don't get rid of me that easy, sweetheart." She smiled. "I'm sure…sure that I want to marry you. We still have a few months before then." She pulled him close again and combed his hair with her fingers. "Do you…is there something that triggers off these dreams or do they just come?"

"Dr. Hayes asked me that. I think as near as I can tell, it's triggered by stress…when I feel threatened, afraid of…."

She waited. When he did not go on, she prompted, "Afraid of…?"

"Losing you…being alone…."

She noticed that his face was wet with tears as he struggled to go on. "Oh, Brett, dear Brett. You don't ever have to worry about losing me. My promise to marry you was forever and ever…no matter what happens in our lives. I don't think I could live without you," she finished tearily.

It was his turn to comfort and he tightened his arms around her. "I love you, kitten…I love you." She lifted her mouth for his kiss.

CHAPTER THIRTY-FOUR

She wasn't aware when she had actually wakened, as she lay contemplating the swiftness of her final semester, the accolades, the scholarship—if she should return to take her master's degree. Guess that decision was no longer hers alone to make—not after today.

She glanced at the bedside clock. Six thirty. Tomorrow when she awakened she would not be alone. The thought sent goose bumps up her arms. She would be Mrs. Brett Walker. Brett...this man that God had sent into her life...this man that had pursued her, protected her, loved her until she couldn't resist...didn't want to resist him. Now he would be hers.

She turned on the lamp and picked up her Bible, turning to the well-marked passages on love and marriage. "O God," she prayed, "help me to be that woman of God...that wife that Brett needs. Help me to love him, honour him, respect him."

❧

Five thirty. Guess I may as well get up; I won't sleep anymore. May as well work out before the day begins. Wonder what I'll be doing at this time tomorrow morning! He grinned as he rolled out of bed and headed to the equipment room. *Wonder if Lee's awake! Better not call her. Won't have to wonder by this time tomorrow.*

He was delighted that they had decided to live in his house...at least until it got too small. He smiled, thinking of little people coming into their lives…a little girl like Lee…whatever would he do with two lovely ladies. Their decision to rent out the Toronto condo, at least for a year, was a good one. Real estate was not a seller's market right now.

And Lee would be back in the office…right next to him…all day…every day. Could a man ask for more? He breathed a prayer of thanks as he laboured on the treadmill.

The course that they had worked through on marriage had been good for him. He never would have considered most of those questions—finances, children, sex, birth control, housing, vehicles, friends, in-laws, health, hobbies, vacations. Each week had been a new revelation. There was more to marriage…and more to Lee…than he had contemplated. He was grateful for all that God had brought into his life. He paused again to tell him so.

The sanctuary had never looked lovelier. Clusters of huge white bells, streamers in varying shades of purple to match the enormous fan-shaped floral arrangements of lilies, iris, and lily-of-the-valley. Bows with lace and tulle to mark the family pews.

He stood at the front, facing the hundreds of guests. He was glad he had chosen a white tuxedo, his groomsmen black. They stood by his side now. All but one. Dave would take his place as best man once he had delivered the bride.

He smiled as one by one the three bridesmaids made their way up the aisle. The first in pale mauve, her matching flowers and ribbons cascading down the front of her gown; the second in a slightly darker tone, the third darker still. Then Sherry…her blonde hair contrasting sharply with the deep purple gown. Each took her appointed place to await the main event.

Suddenly, the strains of the organ reverberated throughout the elegant sanctuary; the guests stood as one. All strained to see as the doors opened, and the little blonde flower girl stepped softly onto the white carpet. Some rose petals caught on her frilly purple gown as she attempted to scatter them. Beside her, in his white tux, her little brother proudly bore the lacy cushion with the wedding band.

Then…there she was! On her brother's arm. Lee! His bride! Her eyes sought his through her veil as she moved slowly up the aisle, her long train flowing gracefully behind her…her deep purple orchids cascading down the front of her elegant silk and lace gown, her hair swept up around the diamond-studded tiara.

They paused as the organ died away. "Who gives this woman to be married to this man?" the pastor asked.

"I do," Dave replied, gently kissing her through the veil. Brett thought his heart would simply burst as he shook hands with Dave. She took his arm. Proudly he escorted her to the altar.

The audience held its collective breath as Scriptural guidelines were given, solos rendered, vows taken, promises made and rings exchanged.

She was his! The future lay ahead of them with its joys and sorrows, hurdles and challenges, defeats and victories…but from now on…from this day forward…they would be there for each other, and more than that…the Lord would be there for both of them!

Will Leanne and Brett live happily ever after?
Watch for the sequel:

Echo of a Dream

Printed in the United States
33641LVS00002B/136-186

9 781413 734515